TASTE

FATIMA MUNROE

TABLE OF CONTENTS

CHAPTER 1
LYRIC

*W*hy this man played with my emotions like he did was beyond my understanding. He knew...HE KNEW he had me in the palm of his hand and he used that to toy with my feelings as much as I allowed him to. But when he had me in the palm of his hand...mmhmm, when he had me cupped in the palm of his hand...his touch was like a switch. With his fingers he flicked me on and off at his every will and I loved it. I fucking loved it...

"How you doing?" the deep voice questioned as I tossed my bag on the back seat of the black car parked at the curb in front of my house. Nolan kept me up all night with his presentation for the big executives at his office that he was due to give tomorrow, so I overslept. I had less than an hour and a half to get to Hartsfield-Jackson airport all the way down in College Park and traffic from Gwinnett County, Georgia was gonna be hell at this time of the day.

"I'm good," I huffed, running my fingers through my hair. If I missed this plane, I might as well forget about that raise because it wasn't happening. "Thad?"

"Yea. Lyric?"

"That's me." His car was clean and smelled good, which I appreciated. Sometimes I got in these people cars and it smelled like they were living out of the back seat. "Can you try to go a little fast? I have a plane to catch."

"I was just about to ask if you were going to the airport," he backed his car up and spoke. "I like to verify addresses before I pull off."

"Oh. Yea."

"Domestic or international?"

"What?"

"Domestic or international. I wanna make sure I drop you off on the right side, the app will take you directly to the international side if you don't specify."

"Oh yea, I forgot the international side is about two miles from the domestic side. I'm flying domestic."

"What airline?"

"Delta please. Thanks for asking."

"No problem," he reassured as we merged onto the interstate. I saw the traffic build-up before we reached the bottom of the ramp. "Shit!" I cussed underneath my breath as the ambulance whizzed by.

The Uber driver turned the radio up and we listened as the announcer warned drivers to stay away from Interstate 85 and find an alternate route. Grabbing my phone, I hopped on the app and began searching for the next flight out to New Orleans. To my surprise, Delta had NOTHING. Same thing when I went to Southwest and American Airlines websites. I'd be damn if I got on a flight from Spirit Airlines, everyone I knew had nothing but horrible things to say about their service. Praise God Jet Blue had something, but it wasn't for another four hours. Guess I had to go to the airport and sit for a while.

"Can you see what's going on?" I crooned my neck to get a glimpse of this accident that had us parked on the interstate like Beyoncé was throwing a concert at the Infinite Energy Center.

"No ma'am, it's too many trucks out here. I can't see nothing."

"Ma'am?" I was taken aback; no he didn't just call me ma'am like he was talking to my grandmother! "How old do you think I am?"

"My mama told me to never insult a woman by asking or trying to guess her age, so I don't know," he answered calmly. "I didn't mean no harm, jus' didn't want to be disrespectful. My apologies."

I studied his features in the rear view mirror. He was a baby; thick curly eyebrows and lashes hovered over his almond shaped eyes. Nose had that African warrior slope, you know the one I'm talking about. Strong and flared slightly at the bottom, the one you loved tracing the outline of as he played sleep on the cool side of the bed. I'm sure he had one of these lil' young girls going crazy with those full, supple lips that he licked every so often. That were also now turned upwards in a playful smirk. "What you looking at?" I frowned, irritated that I got caught daydreaming about his face.

"Nothing. Naw, you know what? I was jus' about to ask you the same question," he chuckled.

"Rude much?" I questioned, pulling up his driver profile on the app. Somebody had to have given him one star.

"I'm a perfect gentleman, if you must know. I jus' felt eyes on me, and when I looked around at the other cars they weren't coming from outside, that's all."

"Hmph," I retorted, scrunching up my nose at his five star rating with over three hundred rides. He was getting one star from me. "If you don't like nobody watching you in the mirror, maybe you should find another profession."

"I like driving. Meet a lot of people this way, actually," he focused back on the road.

"Why you trying to meet people? You don't seem like much of a people person to me."

"I just moved here from Memphis and I don't exactly know where everything is here, so I figured I could make some money and learn the city at the same time," he spoke as we moved up a few inches.

"Memphis, huh?" I smiled, reminiscing on my visit there last year for the blues fest. I had a LOT of fun that weekend. "I love Memphis. You ever been to any of the blues bars there?"

"Yea, I actually play the guitar."

"Oh yea?"

"Mmhmm. Me and my band was supposed to have a permanent gig at a club here, but by the time we moved down and got situated, they found a local band for cheaper," his grip tightened slightly on the steering wheel as he spoke. "So now we done sold all our stuff to move down here and live that Georgia dream for nothing."

"You couldn't get a gig at another club?"

"Nah, our agent had a hard enough time finding us that one. He a good dude though, it wasn't his fault them people was greedy."

"So, do you still play?"

"Yea, I gotta keep my skills up," he smirked. "Couple spots out in Decatur and Stone Mountain let me do a couple of sets here and there when they have like old school Sundays or something. I'll open for whatever band they got out there."

"That's sad," I mumbled absently. Nolan and I were both blessed to land executive positions; I worked as a project manager for Delta while my husband was a VP for a local logistics company. His company relocated him here from Boston and I was blessed with my position once I sent in my resume not too long after we got married. "Atlanta so damn cutthroat, yet people that ain't from here seem to think this the land of milk and honey. Folks move down here all the time like they life 'bout to be so much better and it usually ends up worse."

"I mean, Ma Dukes told me it wasn't the move, but I didn't listen," he sighed once we finally made it halfway to the next exit. "Now she just praying that I get enough money back up to come back home."

"You going back?"

"I ain't gonna lie, sometimes I think about it," he stared at the radio as the voice announced that there was a ninety minute travel time to Buckhead because of the accident. "You want me to come off at the next exit? I know you got a flight to catch."

"Don't worry about the flight, I already took care of that," I waved his words off. "Why would you stay here though?"

"I like a challenge," he replied. "Everything we do in life is based on possibilities. Leaving everything we know to be familiar for the unknown, having a baby, relationships…all that. We go into everything blindly and hope for the best."

"You really think that, huh?" I chuckled, digging in my purse for my phone to check my flight. So far it was still on time.

"Think about it like this: you about to get on an airplane. You don't know if the pilot been drinking or if the plane needs service, all you know is that it's taking you to your destination. You don't focus on the fact that the pilot might fall asleep at the controls, or have a heart attack, or…"

"STOP!" I yelled. He was absolutely correct: I didn't have a copy of this person's clean bill of health. Nor did I know when was the last time the aircraft had a diagnostic check and the results.

"I didn't mean to scare you," he took note of my hand as it shivered with my fingers gripping the sides of the iPhone for dear life. "I'm just making conversation, don't mind me."

"Oh, you fine," I uttered, sitting back in my seat. Watching him focus back on the road as the sheriff directed traffic off the interstate and onto the nearest off ramp, I pondered his statement. Millions of people flew in and out of not just Atlanta, but airports all over the world, and I was positive that out of those millions of people, less than one percent debated whether or not the plane or the person flying the plane was safe. "Uhmm, Thad?"

"Yea."

"I know this is probably gonna sound crazy, but can you…uhhh…can you drive me to New Orleans?"

"Uhmm…"

"I read a story on one of these news websites a while ago about the Uber rider who went from New York to New Jersey by accident, and I saw something recently about some people whose Megabus got stuck in Indianapolis and they had to Uber to Cincinnati, so I know it can be done," I rushed. "I'll pay you."

"How far is New Orleans from here?"

I pulled it up real quick on iMaps. "Around seven hours, give or take a few minutes."

"Seven HOURS? I don't know about all that," he shook his head.

"Oh, your wife might think you cheating huh," I turned my head to stare out the window. "I ain't trying to break up no happy home or nothing."

"No wife. And before you ask, no girlfriend either," he replied. "I'm saying, that's a long ride. Prolly gonna cost you a grip too."

"I'm not worried about the cost. I'm more worried about my personal safety," I spoke truthfully. "You got my mind working overtime now, I'm worried that the plane gonna fall out the sky or something."

"I ain't mean to do all that," he snickered more to himself than me. "That's just stuff I think about sometimes. If it makes you feel a little better, I flew down here myself."

"You don't drive back home when you go?"

"Nah. I ain't getting paid for my time to drive back home, so my patience is a little different."

"I heard that," I chuckled. "So…uhmm…can you?"

"Can I what?"

"Take me to New Orleans?" I questioned hopefully. Not only was Thad cute, but he gave great conversation without being annoying. Maybe later I'd change my mind, but for now I could deal with riding in the car with him for seven hours.

He sighed deeply, I could see him debating on whether or not he wanted to make that ride. "You know what, fuck it. I'll run you out there real quick."

Clapping my hands, I squealed with delight knowing I would be in good hands. "Thank you! And just because I'm the one inconveniencing you, I'll even pay for you a hotel room so you can get some rest before you come back to Atlanta."

"That's cool," he nodded his head, checking his wallet. "I got a couple of dollars to grab some clothes while I'm out there, so we good. I just need you to do one thing for me."

"What's that?"

"Change your destination on the app. I ain't trying to go all the way to Louisiana and only get paid for running you down to the airport."

"Oh, right. I almost forgot," I updated my information. "Can we stop off at the QT and get some snacks?"

"Sure. I need some gas anyway," he replied, turning right at the next light.

CHAPTER 2

Pulling into the QT gas station in Duluth, I smoothed my pencil skirt down briefly as I stepped out of Thad's car. It was still early, so the pumps were semi-packed with landscapers filling up their trucks and power tools, or handymen getting ready for a day of Atlanta traffic. Luckily, we pulled in just as a family pulled away from a pump with their boat in tow, no doubt prepping for a day at Lake Allatoona. I remember back when Nolan and I first got together, we actually met at a party on a houseboat at Lake Lanier. Back when we didn't have to consult our iPhones and schedule a date to be spontaneous. Back when it was more about us and our love than work and building our reputations. I missed those days…

"Can't decide between the spicy nacho Doritos or the sour cream and onion Lays, huh?" Thad's deep tenor vibrated in my ear. Snapping out of my daze, I blinked for a few seconds to focus in on my surroundings. A small Hispanic man was trying his best to stare me out of his walkway, but he was doing a miserable job at it. "Just grab the popcorn."

Taking his advice without a second thought, I grabbed a bag of the white cheddar popcorn and some gummi worms before heading to the register. I already had a bottle of water in my purse and didn't need to spend any extra money at least until we stopped again. Thad motioned for me to cut him in the line, and I didn't hesitate. "Thank you."

"No problem. We need to hurry up and get on the road before I change my mind and drop you back off at home," he smiled. Those dimples coupled with his dentist approved smile had my mind racing with possibilities…what was I talking about? I'm married. Still, it didn't hurt to look.

"Yea, the sooner we hit the interstate the quicker we'll get there, right?" I chuckled, nervously? What was I nervous about? He was just doing his job. I was taking him all the way out of the city, but that's what he signed up for, right? Right.

"Right." We paid for our purchases and he held the door open for me as I strolled to his vehicle. Grabbing the door handle before I could, I shot him a quick smile before climbing in the back seat and making myself comfortable. Plopping in the driver's seat a few seconds later, he started up the car and we began our trip.

"What kind of music do you like to listen to?" he asked, pulling up the Tidal app on his phone.

"Uhmm…can you play some Raheem DeVaughn? That one song…Love Don't Come Easy?"

"Yea, I like him too," Thad replied, searching for the song. A few seconds later I heard his smooth voice as it crooned through the speakers. "Got a whole playlist with him, that new Kenny Lattimore, H.E.R., Music Soulchild,"

"Oh, do you now," I cheesed. "You like listening to that baby making music, huh?"

"After a night of picking folks up and dropping them off without them saying so much as a hello, drunks throwing up in your back seat and getting out like they ain't did nothing, people telling you where to go like they don't hear the GPS, riding through these sketchy neighborhoods…just need something to mellow me out on the ride home, that's all."

I never looked at it from the Uber driver's perspective: with the exception of the sketchy neighborhood thing, he could very easily be talking about me. There was that one night I hung out with a few people from work and had a few too many. Since Nolan wouldn't come get me, I took an Uber. I think I might've thrown up in the car, but I don't remember much from that night other than waking up at my own front door with my key in hand asleep on the porch. When I saw that extra $150 charge from Uber on top of the $10 from my ride, I hit the roof! Ready to cuss out whoever answered the phone along with their supervisor if need be, they told me the driver provided them with pictures and a brief narrative of my ride the night before. Meekly, I thanked them for the clarification before hanging up the phone.

"Well, that makes sense," I shifted timidly in my seat. We both got quiet, listening to the music and lost in our own thoughts. I pulled out my iPad and hot spot to catch up on some reports at work while he merged back onto I-85 South.

"Can you focus on…me." I heard coming lowly from the front seat. "Baby can you focus…on meeee?" Thad was singing along with H.E.R.'s single, 'Focus'. I raised my head slightly, looking down my black, horn rimmed frames at the back side of the waves circling around the crown of his head. For a second I thought…no, I secretly hoped…he was talking to me.

Hands in the soap

Have the faucet's running and I keep looking at you
Stuck on the phone and you're stuck in your zone
You don't have a clue…

He really doesn't have a clue though, I thought back to the brief interaction with my husband of ten years earlier today before I ran out the house. Nolan was asleep when I tiptoed out of bed and hopped in the shower. Quickly lathering myself up, I waited for him to peek in the bathroom so we could get a quickie before I left on a business trip that would take me away from him for the next three days. I needed that from him, and judging by the way his morning wood poked me in the back when my eyes popped open this morning, he needed it just as bad as I did. Some thick, soapy dick would've hit the spot this morning.

Instead, I found myself in the bathroom alone as I lathered my long, thick dreads that just began to graze my perfectly round bottom; thanks to two hundred squats per day. I missed Nolan; and the crazy part was that he was only a few feet away. He wasn't cheating on me, the private investigator and hidden cameras throughout the house confirmed that. Nolan really and truly just worked too much, and it was sad. Sad that I had to get my bunny out and relieve myself yet again before a business trip when

I had a whole husband that should've had my face smashed against the glass in our shower stall while he dug my guts out.

"You ok back there?" Thad's voice interrupted my thoughts.

"Uhmm, yea I'm good," I replied. "Going over some work and this one report makes absolutely no sense, that's all."

"Comfortable? It's not too hot, is it?"

"No, it's fine. Slightly cool, just the way I like it. Can I crack a window if it gets stuffy?"

"Sure. Make yourself comfortable."

"Thanks." Turning back to my iPad as we passed the sign welcoming us to Alabama, I secretly wondered if Thad would mind me pulling out my remote controlled vibrator so I could get one off real quick. *He did say for me to make myself comfortable,* I snickered to myself, pushing my glasses back up on the bridge of my nose.

CHAPTER 3
THAD

Regardless of what she said, Lyric couldn't possibly be a day over thirty. I'd even give her thirty-one if that was her mood for today. Either way, whether she was thirty or forty, I'd slide her this young wood as soon as she gave me the green light to do so.

My Uber days usually started at night. I'd turn on the app anywhere between 12 and 2 a.m., and drive until around 8 or 9, right after rush hour traffic. Last night though, I slept through my alarm and didn't get out until around 5 a.m. My cousin who also drove, told me that I had a better chance of making some money if I went north, and after I dropped the stripper that I picked up from Blue Flame off at home, I did just that. I was just about to turn back around when I caught Lyric's request for a ride ten minutes from where I was. Sometimes the app gets turned around in these subdivisions, so I was glad to see it take me straight to her front door.

Usually I don't get out to help people with their luggage, they knew how heavy it was when they packed it. After all, I'm not escorting them inside the airport, so they needed to get used to that weight. After she slammed the trunk shut, I hit the automatic locks on my Ford Taurus and waited for her to get in. Glancing in the rear view mirror briefly, I saw she wasn't a complete swamp monster, and when I caught her watching me, I licked my lips to give her a show. She was sexier than I thought she was. I was looking forward to this trip.

New Orleans though? Definitely wasn't expecting that one. It was all good; I had people out there so I wasn't concerned with nobody trying to rob me for the whip, but had I known when I left the house this morning that I'd be in N.O. that evening, I would've packed a bag. In hindsight, it WAS my fault. I called myself making small talk and it ended up with me taking a sexy, total stranger to the Big Easy, a city best known for Mardi Gras and beignets, trap stars and the type of women who only came out at night. Some sexy ass women, but the headache wasn't worth the risk.

Wondering if she was gonna give me cash or swipe a card for the hotel once we got to the city, I was trying to remember if Trenaé's number was still saved in my phone so I could surfboard THAT pussy before I came back. Now she was a good girl in public; when I met her she was enrolled at Grambling State and in the last year of her doctorate program in education. Coming from a two-parent household, I remember everybody that knew her always held her to a higher standard than most, like she was gonna come save little black kids in the hood. They didn't know Trenaé like I knew Trenaé though: the Trenaé I knew loved being pounded from the back with a braided cord made up of her school colors wrapped around her throat and pulled tightly. The Trenaé I knew loved for me to sit her up on top of the balcony railing on the second floor of her parents' plantation style home overlooking Lake Pontchartrain and eat that kat while she balanced precariously over the edge with the sun coming up over the water. I had to see if her number was still in my phone the next time we stopped.

"Thad," a gentle voice breezed against the back of my neck. "Can I make a request?"

"Sure. What you need?"

"Can you change the music to some John Coltrane or someone? I need to concentrate, and Maxwell got me back here singing along with him and those pretty wings," she giggled.

"Yea, no problem." I removed my phone from the holder attached to the vent and handed it to her. "Go ahead and turn to whatever you wanna hear."

"Where did you go just then?" she questioned with her head down in the phone's screen.

"What do you mean?"

"Looked like you zoned out for a minute. Is everything ok?"

"Yea, I'm fine. Just thinking about something that happened a few years ago, you know how that goes."

"Unfortunately I do," she spoke longingly, removing the glasses from her pretty, heart shaped face to turn and look out the window at the road passing by. Sighing deeply, she perched the frames back to their spot on the bridge of her nose and shook her head. "Can't go home again though, can you?" she mumbled under her breath, finally settling on a song by Celine Dion.

"Depends on your definition of home."

"You know what I mean," she sighed, exasperated. "Home. Where everything is happy, where you feel safe. Where everything is…"

"Predictable?"

"Not necessarily predictable," she shook her head slowly as she scrunched up her face in an attempt to collect her thoughts. "More so where everything is familiar."

"Lyric, you married?"

"I am."

I glanced briefly at her in the rear view mirror to get a sense of her angst. "Happily?"

"I used to think so, but now…" her voice trailed off as she turned her attention to the window.

"Now?"

"I'm not so sure."

"Why not?"

Shifting her focus back to inside the car, I saw her fidget with her hands as she struggled again to find the right words. "Nolan is a good man," she began.

"But?"

"What makes you think there's a 'but'?"

"You not happy. Woman as beautiful as you should always be happy." I shifted my eyes back to focus on the road.

"What's that supposed to mean?" she questioned shyly from the back seat.

"Honestly?"

"Yea."

"Lyric, you're perfection. Chocolate brown eyes that match that chocolate brown skin, you ain't got no fat on you, got that ass bouncing just right when you walk. Don't even get me started on your thighs and them pretty ass legs."

"You noticed all that from me sitting back here in the back seat?"

"Nah, I saw all that when you got out and smoothed that skirt down at the gas station. Why you think I let you get in front of me in the line? Every man in there was imagining you naked, you even had Puerto Rican papi in there licking his lips. Yea I had to snatch you up before somebody in there did."

"Damn, really?" she snickered in her palm. "I didn't see any of that."

"Mmhmm. If your husband don't see that, I feel sorry for him." I turned the air conditioning up a little; it was beginning to get warm in the car and it wasn't coming from the front seat. "You mind if I come off at this next exit?"

"Why we coming off the road?"

"I gotta pee," I replied, steering my car towards the ramp. There was a Pilot truck stop a half mile down the road on the right and they had some pretty decent food depending on who was behind the counter cooking it.

"Me too," she wiggled in her seat as we parked in front of the building. Soon as I put the car in park, she jumped out and ran inside looking around for the bathroom.

The store was quiet, I'm assuming because it was the middle of the day and the location was so remote. Taking care of my hygiene, I washed my hands and headed out of the bathroom. Stepping inside the convenience store, I grabbed a small cup of pineapples for me to munch on while on the road. Passing the women's restroom on my right side before I walked out of the building, I heard what sounded like someone crying. Never the type of man to leave a woman helpless, I tapped on the door to make sure she was ok. "Everything aight in there?"

"Yea…yes, Thad I'm…I'm ok," Lyric replied shakily.

"Lyric? You sure? I'm coming in to check on you," I called out gently while opening the door slowly, stepping inside cautiously. "You in here by yourself?"

"Ahhh…I…mmmm….I think so,"

"Am I interrupting something?" I turned the deadbolt on the door and pushed the garbage can against it just in case. I didn't need to catch no case out here in the country, but Lyric sounded like…

Checking underneath the stalls for her feet, I saw one of her stilettos planted firmly on the floor with her pink lace thong around her ankle in the handicapped stall. Hearing her heavy breathing led me to the only conclusion feasible: Lyric was in the bathroom stall at the Pilot gas station fingering that sloppy, wet pussy. I heard her fingers as they eased in and out of her slit, my ears picked up her tiny moans each time her fingers plunged inside. SHIT! The whole damn bathroom smelled like that sweet honey and I wanted to taste that juice on my lips.

"Nooo…mmmm…Thad you…you…."

"Unlock the door, baby," I mumbled lowly, jiggling the door slightly.

"I…I can't…"

"Yes, you can. Raise your free hand up and lean forward. Slide the lock to your right," I coached, hearing her follow my direction as the door to the stall swung open. "That's a big girl," I mumbled, joining her quick session. "Daddy so proud of you. Lemme give you a present for being my big girl," I ran my free hand through her dreads as my hand found her sugary spot. Resting my growing rod against her stomach, I tickled her stickiness as she moved back and forth against my two fingers, moaning in ecstasy. Tilting her head to the right, I ran my tongue down the side of her neck, the salty taste of her skin had me ready to slide inside her softness. Her heat told me she wanted me, feeling her cream pool in my palm I gently bit her shoulders while she whimpered for me to stroke that kitty some more.

"Thad…mmmm…."

BAM! BAM! BAM! "Hey, you gotta open this door, it's people out here that gotta pee too!" a woman's voice yelled with a country twang. "What you doing in there anyway, lady!"

"Fuck me on the road, Thad. Please?" Lyric begged, ignoring the store clerk. "I need you to…"

BAM! BAM! BAM! "I'ma call the po-lice if 'un you don't come outta there by the time I count to five! One…two…"

"Let's go, baby. I don't need to get locked up because yo' fine ass in here trying to get some dick." I pulled her skirt back down around her ass. Picking up her panties from the cold tiled floor, I stuffed them in my pocket as she rushed to move the garbage can and open the door.

"I was sick," she explained hurriedly, rushing past the clerk and running to the car as I slouched out behind her.

"Yea she was sick and I had to give her some medicine. You need some too?" I grabbed my dick and licked my lips at the skinny white girl with the big titties glaring at me.

She sucked in her breath and grabbed her chest before running her tongue across her teeth slowly. "Call me," she whispered, grabbing my arm briefly. "I'm here every day until five."

"My services ain't free, I drive for Uber in Atlanta."

"I'll pay you," she called out hoarsely to my back.

I had no plans on coming back out here for no pussy, but it was always funny to me to see these country women fall in love with this dick. "I'll call you soon as I drop her off."

CHAPTER 4

I took my time walking back to the car with Lyric sitting in the back seat with her eyes watching my every move like a hawk. My dick swung left to right in my grey sweatpants as I approached, and Lyric was definitely pleased. She wanted me to fuck her on the road; I wondered if that meant at a hotel on the way, or actually pulled over on the side of the interstate.

"Grabbed you some pineapples," I reached across the back seat and held the fruit out in her direction. "I wanna taste that pussy next."

"Can you taste it now?" she pleaded with one hand up her skirt as she took the fruit from my hand, sliding a cube of the sweet treat inside her. "Bet it's real good now," she purred, flicking her tongue before biting a second cube while letting the juice run down her lips. Starting the car up, I pulled out of the gas station and onto the side road leading us back to the interstate. "We can pull over on the side of the road and turn on the hazard lights, like we caught a flat or something. Please, Thad?"

"I thought you had a husband," I replied, pulling over to the side of the road and turning on my hazards. "He ain't tonguing down that fat pussy between your legs?"

"Nope," she whimpered. Glancing quickly in my rear view, I saw her writhing in her seat with excitement. "She need it too, don't she?"

"Mmhmm. She ready."

Turning around before I let my seat back, I saw Lyric had already hiked her skirt up and had that pussy already talking as she manipulated her clit; alternating between rubbing the fruit up and down her slit and sliding her thin, well-manicured fingers inside as the juices flowed out. Spreading her legs open a little wider, I listened to the window whine as the automatic switch allowed it to roll down halfway while watching her slipping as she tried to control that orgasmic explosion. Leaning the seat back as far as it would go, I saw her head tilt backwards as her lips formed a cherry red O before she ran her tongue across her teeth. That shit was sexy as fuck.

Replacing her fingers with mine, I gingerly fingered her clit while licking her fingers clean. Scooting her ass forward some, seeing her ass cheeks sitting underneath her honeypot as it slowly wept sweet cum, I was more than ready to slide my tongue deep inside her slit. Gripping her waist tightly, I gently tilted her hips upwards, taking a moment to inhale the sweet scent of pineapples and lust that saturated her pussy. Baby was still cumming slowly and I hadn't touched her like I wanted to yet.

"Who pussy this is, baby?" I spoke, separating the pink lips of her clit before dragging my tongue from the bottom to the top of her sticky, lapping her juices slowly while sucking the pineapple out before sliding two fingers inside of her love volcano.

"Hmmm…yours…" she whined, writhing with pleasure. "Yours, Thaddeus," she grinded her pussy against my beard while I turned my head to the right slightly to get a better angle while I tongue kissed her love. Pulling her closer, I got a better grip around her ass as I gingerly dragged my teeth across her clit, moaning while sliding my tongue in and out of her clit.

"Suck my dick, Lyric," I commanded, coming up briefly for air. Freeing up my left hand as she climbed into the sixty-nine position, I hurriedly snatched him out of my jogging pants as she perched spread eagle on top of my face. Wrapping her hand around my shaft, she spit on the tip and deep throated him with pleasure. I felt my dick head slide down her throat as her stomach tightened and contracted; she was choking on my shit and trying not to throw up in the process. That gag reflex kicked in quick, and it only made her mouth wetter, making my dick harder each time she bobbed her head.

"You taste so sweet," she mumbled between strokes, lapping up the pre-cum I felt traveling up the underside on my dick only moments before. Lyric's tongue moved down the length of the vein as her lips sucked the bulbous tip of my shit; she wanted that explosion from me as bad as I wanted it from her. Sticking a finger in her puckered other hole, I flicked my tongue furiously across her clit, trying to make her cum while she tugged on my balls and squeezed my meat trying to get the same from me.

"Lyriiiiic, stop muthafuckin' playing and suck that shit like a Jolly…oooo, that feel good," I ain't gon' flex, she felt my dick brick up and popped her lips right back on him, swallowing him whole. Ain't no woman ever did that to me, I was trying to see what that felt like. Wrapping both arms around her waist with a death grip, I wrapped my mouth around her clit, fucking her slit with my tongue as she let that hurt from her husband go all over my face.

"THADDEUS! OH SHIT, GIMME THAT DICK!" she screamed as I exploded in her mouth. Gripping the back of her head to hold her still, I fucked her face while spurting my thick, creamy nut down her throat. Oh, but she wasn't done yet, my dick heard her when she begged for him to be inside that wet pussy.

"Squat that pussy on yo' dick, girl," I ordered, and she quickly complied, swallowing my cum. Plopping down with a wet squish, she rode my shit like a champ, as best as she could considering we were in the driver's seat of a Ford Taurus. Resting one of her knees on the armrest, she turned sideways and balanced herself with one hand on the steering wheel and the other on my chest. Bouncing her scalding hot pussy on my shit, I tried to control the situation as the tip of my shit beat the bottom of her fat, juicy berry.

"My dick, Thaddeus…mmmm, this MY DICK, THADDEUS," she yelled. "FUCK THIS SHIT, BABY! HIT THIS MUTHAFUCKIN' PUSSY!"

Seizing her shoulders while she was in mid twerk, I held her still as I shoved my meat deep inside of her walls. "Got this shit wet like a fuckin' water moccasin for me, don't you? Mmhmm…you want me to hit this muthafuckin' pussy, huh? Hit this muthafuckin' pussy Lyric? Like that?" I growled, sweat pouring off of me as I pounded her sweltering, steamy box. "Come on, girl, say something. Keep talking that shit, you making my dick hard. GIMME THIS MUTHAFUCKIN' PUSSY!"

Lyric's words caught in her throat while I banged her pussy like she should've been fucked all along. The trucks speeding past rocked the car side to side slightly as I got in her shit and destroyed any hope her husband had of getting her back, ever. Why all the good pussy married to a weak nigga that don't know how to treat a queen?

She gave it to me; that pussy rain that I was looking for. I felt her shit open up around my pole like a lotus flower slowly opening at that first ray of sunlight as she rained that orgasm on my dick and balls. I was right behind her; feeding that aquatic bloom by shooting cum deep inside of her womb. Leaning in to bite her neck, I sat my dick deep down inside of her as she wept real tears gently rubbing her clit against my rod. "Thaddeus…."

"Yea, baby?"

"I…I…mmmm…"

"Let it go, baby. Tell Daddy."

"Thank you for letting me cum. You were amazing," she kissed me on my cheek before climbing down from my dick. Not the words I expected, but we still had four hours to go.

"You welcome, sexy. Need to go back to the truck stop and get cleaned up?"

"Umm, yea. Everything on me is sticky," she giggled shyly.

"Aight." Letting my seat back up, I started the car up and got off at the next exit so I could turn around. An awkward silence settled between us as we rode the mile back to the Pilot truck stop. Parking on the side of the building, I wiped myself off with the wipes in my glove compartment before popping my trunk and grabbing the cleaning supplies I kept underneath the spare tire. I wasn't going back in, Jenny might try and come from behind the counter on me.

"I'll…uhmm…I'll only be a few minutes," she gave me a tight smile before rushing inside the building. I knew fucking one of my riders was a bad idea, but it was too late now.

CHAPTER 5
LYRIC

He wasn't supposed to be that good, I mumbled to my reflection in the mirror. Silk flowers adorned the double sinks on both sides in the public restroom as I absently pushed the soap dispenser while silently cussing myself out. Thaddeus was bigger than my husband, sucked pussy a thousand times better, and his stroke game was miraculous, phenomenal…oh my God! Incredible! Who knew Uber drivers was out here slinging good dick like that? Certainly not me.

Each time I ran the stiff, wet paper towel across my pussy lips, Thad's face popped up in my head. *How am I supposed to ride to New Orleans in this man's back seat, knowing I wanna sit my pussy on his lap and kiss his face as he drove?* SHIT! I should've never gave in to temptation. I should've had enough willpower to stop sneaking stares at him in the rear-view mirror. I should've stopped inhaling the air inside his car, which smelled like the Black Magic velvet pine tree hanging from the car's interior. It smelled like Ralph Lauren Polo, the cologne Nolan wore before he moved up the ranks and settled into a cushy career as a vice president. Only problem with that was that on Thad it smelled better, more masculine. It smelled like we should be fucking. Hard and long, just like Thaddeus' love stick annihilating my insides as I begged him to go deeper.

Digging the small bottle of Scope from the bottom of my purse, I took a swig so my breath didn't smell like dick when I spoke to someone. Secretly I didn't mind, I loved Thad's dick. Mmm…he tasted so good. His cum was fruity with a citrusy aftertaste, I could gargle on that shit for the rest of my life. I wanted to feel those soft lips that he pressed against my pussy lips on top of my other lips, wanted to do to his tongue what I did to his dick with my hands wrapped gently around his neck. I had to be ready when I got back in the car…ready to resist the temptation that I got from those waves circling around his head and making me seasick. He knew what he was doing when he came out the house this morning.

"Lyric, we gotta go, sweetheart," Thad's voice called out lovingly from the other side of the door. I wasn't divorcing my husband because he gave me the security of my current lifestyle. I wondered if Thad would be ok with being my side piece.

Get it together, Lyric. This man isn't your forever love, Nolan is. All couples go through it, go home and tell your man what you need from him. Forget about Thaddeus.

"Coming, Thad," I replied, running my fingers through my dreads for inspiration. I had to do something before I divorced my husband of ten years over some good dick. Some REAL good dick.

Smoothing the wrinkles from my skirt and adjusting my shirt, I checked the mirror one last time to make sure I didn't look as disheveled as I did when I burst through those doors and made a beeline for the restroom. Thad had that effect on me already; I could still feel his hands wrapped around my waist as he demanded I suck his dick. I had no other choice but to comply and I was glad I did. Running my tongue quickly across my front teeth, I pulled the door opened and strutted out the exit with my head held high and pussy jumping. Laying eyes on him again, my heart pounded in my chest. *Calm down, Lyric. Leave this man alone.*

Reaching for the door handle on the back door, I saw Thad move towards me from my peripheral vision and cussed under my breath. "We a little bit more than driver and rider, right? Come sit up front with me."

No Lyric. Don't do it. "Ok," my pussy answered for me as my mind screamed for me to stop. Smiling brightly as he held my door opened, I climbed in and made myself comfortable as he walked around the back of the car to the other side and got in.

"Thank you, huh," he began as we merged onto the interstate for the third time. I was beginning to wonder if we'd even make it to New Orleans anytime this week.

"Huh?"

"Thank you?"

"What you mean?"

"Aye, I don't have sex with my passengers, just so you know," he fixed his eyes on the road. "Contrary to what you might think, this ain't just a lil' job; I make a living off this money until something more permanent comes along."

"Who said anything about…"

"Lyric, that whole 'thank you' thing? Like it was more of a business transaction than what it was? Like you better than me," he grumbled. "I might be driving you out here, but I ain't the help."

"Thad it ain't…"

"You know what, maybe it's me. Maybe I'm the one making this out to be more than what it is. Maybe you should ride in the back."

"Wait, wait, wait. Let's talk about this, ok? I never said you were beneath me, I just said thank you to be polite. I mean, what do you say to your Uber driver after he just gave you some of the best dick you've had in six months? 'Now that's what I call a five-star ride, I'll tip you on the app'?"

"Six months? Damn girl, that's why that pussy was so wet," he snickered while sliding a hand under my skirt. "Scoot that pussy up some."

I did as I was told so he could finger my pussy while he drove. His thick digits were a tease, I wanted some more dick. "Thad, whyyyyy…."

"Shut the fuck up an' wrap them lips back around my dick head." I don't know why, but every time he was aggressive with me it made my pussy jump. "Prove to me you want this dick."

Leaning over the armrest, I opened my mouth, fully prepared to do his bidding. Without warning, he grabbed the back of my neck and shoved my head down in his lap, moving my head to his rhythm.

"I'm the Uber man, now, huh. I wasn't the Uber man when you was painting my dick white though, was I?" he growled. His roughness had the opposite affect on me; my body was on fire and my pussy was about to explode for the sixth time in an hour. Nolan never fucked me like this. "ANSWER ME, LYRIC!" he thundered, pulling me up by my neck while his cum shot in the air like a water fountain across my lips.

"You my man, Thaddeus," I cried in lust, rubbing his slippery syrup across my lips before lapping him up. You not the Uber man, baby."

"You thank your man for giving you dick?"

"No," I stuck my tongue out to lick the tip again, but he wouldn't let me. Thad was punishing me, and I loved it.

"Then yo' muthafuckin' ass bet not say that shit to me again then, got dammit," he directed sternly.

"Ok, baby," I whispered sultrily. "Ok. Can I have some more? Please?"

"I'll think about it when we get to Mississippi," he pushed me back to my side of the car. "For now, play with that pussy and think about that shit you pulled."

"But Thad…"

"I'm Thad now?" he raised an eyebrow at me. "When you was riding this dick, I was Daddy."

"Daddy, I won't do it again, I promise."

CHAPTER 6

We were about fifteen minutes from Mississippi, but he didn't say which side of the state: the Alabama side or the Louisiana side. So I was in the middle of playing peek-a-boo pussy and giving him a show when my phone rang.

"Don't answer it," he instructed, playing with his dick with one hand as he snuck glimpses of my private show every now and then.

"I-I gotta get that, it might be work." Reaching in the back seat, I found my purse and dug the phone from its resting spot at the bottom of the bag. "Hello?"

"Lyric?"

"Hey…" I tugged at my skirt with one hand while balancing the phone in the crook of my neck. My eyes darted quickly between Thad and my sweaty palms as I focused on my husband's voice. "…baby. How are you, my love?"

"I was just calling to check on you since I haven't heard from you. Is everything ok?"

"Yea…every…everything's fine," I tried not to sound flustered, but I was failing miserably. "How did your presentation go?"

"Oh you know I wow'ed 'em!" he gushed as Thad pulled the car over again. "My boss was floored when he saw the slide you told me to add in, I think that's what got us the account. I was calling to tell you thanks babe. I don't know where I'd be without you."

"Aww, you're welcome love. That's what wives are for, right?" I cheered as Thad leaned over and sucked on my neck.

"I know I've been distant, but that's gonna change, ok? Maybe we can start working on that baby we've been talking about?"

"Mmm, I like that," I said to both men. *When did I become a hoe, though?*

"Can't wait to see you in New Orleans, babe. We can get started on that tonight, what hotel are you at again?" my husband growled sexily in my ear as Thad unbuttoned my blouse. Staring longingly into my orbs, he unhooked the front clasp on my bra with one flick of his finger, allowing my full breasts freedom from their captor. I felt my mouth open slightly as he lifted my melons towards his lips, lazily caressing my mahogany areolas with the tip of his tongue.

"I want you so bad," I ran my hand across Thad's waves with my breath caught in my throat. He grabbed my hand and placed it on top of his long, thick member, never breaking eye contact. I was this man's own personal celestial body, and his touch would have me singing his name to the heavens in a few moments.

"You deserve to have orgasms, Lyric," Thad whispered in my ear. "You deserve to cum every day, three times a day at the least. Don't let this garbage muthafucka have you believing you should tolerate mediocre dick because y'all married. If your pussy was trash, he'd find better, so you do better."

Got dammit, Thad was right. My pussy had to be 'bout something, Nolan was still sniffing around. He almost had me believing I was supposed to use my toys since he wasn't fucking me on a regular. "Mmm…I know you do," Nolan's voice in my ear broke me out of my trance. "You know what? Lemme find something flying out within the next couple of hours. What time is your meeting tomorrow?"

"Huh…uhmm…Nolan…"

"I know you need to release, don't you? Pussy tight too…you gonna walk in that meeting in the morning feeling like the CEO," he teased. He was right about one thing: I was definitely walking in that meeting feeling like I owned a majority share of Delta stock.

"I'm sorry love, you caught me at a bad time. Lemme call you back, a bunch of us going out…uuuuhhh…" I moaned uncontrollably at Thad biting my nipple.

"Even out of town, business is still business, right babe?" Nolan observed dismally. "Go ahead, I know how it goes. Call me later, ok?"

"Mmhmm…" I called out before he hung up.

Did I feel bad that my husband wanted to share his good news with me and I was being loved on by someone else? Somewhat. I've come home more than a few times with great news about something that happened at work and Nolan fell asleep on me. Our marriage wasn't on the rocks but judging from the way Thad couldn't keep his hands off me, maybe it was. I wondered if Uber was ok with him making all these stops while we got in quickies up and down Interstate 85. They probably didn't care, long as they got their cut.

"I ain't never shared nothing in my life; not clothes, shoes, hell I don't share my muthafuckin' food. Next time he call tell him it's over," Thad insisted, adjusting his seat before starting the car up.

Buttoning my blouse, I nodded my head and wondered what kind of twisted web I was weaving, cheating on my husband. Was it worth it? "I'm gonna get in the back seat so I can take a nap." Not waiting for a response, I opened my door while smoothing my shirt flat for the millionth time, as if the cars swooshing by knew what I was doing with my Uber driver. Guilt was starting to set in, and I didn't like it one bit. Hopefully, Thad would drive straight through so I could salvage a piece of my dignity.

CHAPTER 7
THAD

I didn't mean to be hard on her, but I didn't like her talking to her husband. I understood she was married, and this might've been a way for her to let off some steam, but it was something about her…something about her that I needed. Something about her that was missing in my life. Whatever it was, I wasn't letting go of that easy.

Glancing in the mirror every so often, I saw Lyric in the back seat sleeping peacefully. I wanted to be the one she woke up and gave that sleepy, confused look before the smile that came right behind it, knowing I was the one responsible for the early morning ache between her thighs. I wanted to be the warmth that filled the space in her bed currently occupied by her husband, only I wasn't sharing. I wanted Lyric all to myself. Fuck that, I NEEDED Lyric all to myself.

Baby must've been tired because she slept all the way to New Orleans, she didn't even wake up when I stopped that last time for some gas. Nudging the leg gingerly tucked underneath her in the back seat, she woke up slowly, looking around absently as she stretched. I gave her a few minutes to get acclimated. "We're here."

"Where?"

"This is the address you keyed in on the app."

"Oh, this is nicer than I thought it would be," she opened her door before I could get to her, stepping out and standing at the curb of the small house on the side street. "Yea this is real nice. Mmhmm."

"You staying with family?"

"No, I found this on AirBnb's website, I hate staying in hotels when I go out of town," she stated, rounding the back of the car for her luggage. "Pop the trunk for me?"

"I got it," I mused, shoo-ing her away from my car. "So you don't wanna stay in a hotel, but you gonna put me in one though, huh."

"You can stay here too," she stepped cautiously over the concrete curb heading up the walkway. "It's a one bedroom that sleeps four."

"And your husband on his way down here? Nah. I'm good love, enjoy," I snickered, grabbing her bag from the trunk. "Speaking of hubby, how he don't know you don't like hotels? I heard him ask which hotel you at."

"I have no idea," she sighed. "Maybe because he wasn't paying attention when I told him the story about when that one place had bed bugs, even though they were supposed to be 'five stars' too."

"Oh, you definitely ain't putting me in no roach motel out here masquerading as the Four Seasons," I chuckled, walking behind her as she headed to the house. "I'll sleep on the road first!"

"Now why would I put my lover in a…what you call it? Roach motel?" she sniggled, turning around to palm the side of my face. "No, baby, I booked you a room around the corner in the French Quarter."

"French Quarter, huh." The Louisiana heat was thick with anticipation in front of the small house near Canal Street as I closed the space between us to connect her full lips to mine. "So, is this it?"

"What do you mean," she spoke more of a statement, slipping me some tongue as I went in for a second taste.

"I just drove you out here to drop you off, now we done?" I secured my hands around her wide hips, our bodies attracted each other like ants to honey. The fire we made raged in my soul; looking in her eyes I saw that flame burning brightly in the center of her pupils.

"Thaddeus," she placed her hand gently in the center of my chest, "you knew I was married…"

I took her lips in mine, our tongues circled together in a tantric dance between two lovers who couldn't survive without the other. Leaning on the front door of the small structure, I ran my hand up her skirt, my hands squeezing her thigh as she slid her leg up at a ninety-degree angle. Grinding against my manhood, Lyric started peck kissing my chest through my white tee, making my dick jump. "Mmmm…calm down baby, you next," she whispered, rubbing him through my jogging pants.

"Our chemistry is off the chain, Lyric. You can't tell me it ain't. You gonna give up us for your husband?"

"Thad," Lyric sighed. "We took vows. You know what that means?"

"Means you married. I get it."

"No, honey," she put her leg down and fixed her skirt. "It means that no matter what, we're in this. We're a team. Nolan was sent to me by God for me…"

"I'on wanna hear that shit, Lyric! Your husband was sent to you by God, who sent me then, the devil? Fuck outta here! Yea, you part of a team aight, Team Good Pussy!" She snatched away from me, reaching into the mailbox attached to the house for the key and I followed her, my nostrils flaring. "How you gonna let me hit that wet this whole ride, now we here an' all of a sudden you married?"

"I'll text you the address to where you'll be staying and tip you on the app!" She snatched her luggage away and fumbled with the key in the lock. "We had fun, but now it's over. Stay away from me, Thaddeus."

I stared at her, watching her lips move yet not wanting to hear nothing she said. Now it was stay away from her, but just a few hours ago it was 'I need you,' 'I love you', 'Don't leave me.' Damn, when those same words used to roll off my tongue to the opposite sex, I never thought twice about deleting her number after I got what I wanted. Here I was with the tables turned on me by a thick, sexy, MARRIED woman and it was some bullshit. A part of me told me to kick the door down and give her this stroke so she would get her mind right and leave with me. Stepping backwards down the walkway so I could make sure she got in the house safely, I nodded my head in the direction of the front door as she slammed it behind her. "Not a problem, Lyric," I nodded to the ghosts whispering their stories of old New Orleans on the breeze blowing lightly through the mature trees framing the small cottage.

CHAPTER 8

Trenaé's number was still in my phone; I found it as I rode to the address Lyric sent me to where I'd be staying for the evening. I hit her line and as soon as she answered, I hung up. I wasn't in the mood for her freak nasty ass tonight. It was funny, because for the first time I was in New Orleans and didn't wanna hit up the club, didn't wanna go on the French Quarter, didn't wanna do shit. What I wanted to do was Lyric.

Funny thing about men that a lot of women don't know: we really ain't hard to please. Now the thing that has women constantly trying to figure us out is because what they fail to realize is that no matter how much pussy she give up, no matter how freaky she is, no matter how clean she keep the house and the kids, we only gonna be faithful to that one who we feel is worth us being faithful to. That's not on her, it's on US.

As a man, Lyric's husband should be a part of her makeup kit, because a man that makes his woman happy on a daily basis gives her a natural glow that makeup can't and the world can see it. I would've never had her legs wrapped around my neck if that was the case. The opportunity would've never presented itself.

Lyric was in my soul; she got in my head in a matter of hours. A man looks for that woman who is on her path of growth and evolution to be his partner on their journey through life together. Their souls unite daily to create a space full of love, healing and awareness; we experienced a transition together which brought us both to this point in time. I felt it, when she opened up and gave me that orgasm, she gave me a piece of herself and I did the same.

The room she reserved for me at the house in the French Quarter was small. In addition to the bed there was a small antique dresser with a mirror, a nightstand, an old, worn chair that looked like the house was built around it, and a television sitting on milk crates covered up with a thin sheet. There was no air conditioning, and the ceiling fan was on its last leg. Stepping into the closet sized bathroom that looked more like an afterthought, I slid sideways into the tight shower stall and washed Lyric and the road off my body.

I wanted her here with me, those big titties of hers mushed against my chest as we lathered one another in the compacted space. Grabbing my dick, I imagined she was here with me, whispering in my ear how she wanted me to go deeper, harder, faster and make that pussy cum. Squeezing the base of my shit, I rotated my hips back and forth imagining my palm was her hot pocket, her walls closed in and inhaled my girth as I moved deeper and deeper…

"Sssss…fuck that shit, baby," I moaned in her phantom ear with my arm on the wall in front of me, resting my head against my forearm. "I love you, Lyric…I love you. Can I have you, love? I need you, Lyric," I whined, exploding my seed on the metallic wall as my mind told me she wasn't here in reality. "Shit."

I finished my evening ritual, watching as my potential kids floated down the drain, never to be realized as the great people that they could've become. If only the woman who was worthy in my eyes to carry my children full term was here, we could be doing what it took to create a life, not me asking her if she was ok with us working on a baby. Nolan was a pussy; a real man keeps his woman so happy she don't have a problem giving him babies. Not 'we'll think about it,' not later on down the line in their marriage. That was part of their union; if he was letting her run him like that, I see why I got the pussy. Yea, happy wife happy life, but no woman wants a man that'll let her walk all over him. I'll give her what she want, but I still gotta have her in check. Balance is an important part of any relationship.

Laying across the bed with my hands behind my head as I stared at the worn antique paint peeling from the ceiling after lotioning myself up, I gave thought to her words. 'Stay away from me, Thad.' I didn't want to, but I also wasn't a stalker. If Lyric wanted me to stay away from her, that's what I'd do, but it would take a while to forget her completely.

Hearing my phone vibrate somewhere near the window, I grabbed it and stared at the screen; Trenaé was ringing my phone back. I wasn't even in the mood to hear what kind of freaky intentions she had tonight; as a matter of fact it was time for me to delete her number. "Hello?"

"Hi, I…uhhh…I got a call from this number earlier?"

"Oh, my bad sweetheart, I called the wrong number."

"You sure? This Trenaé."

"Yea I'm sure."

"You wanna make it the right number? Just for tonight?"

"Nah."

"Lemme send you a pic, maybe that'll help," she volunteered.

"No need," I heard a beep in my ear alerting me to a message. "Wife just changed her number and I mixed up the last four digits."

"I'm married too, what your spouse don't know won't hurt her," she purred. "What's your name?"

Married? It hadn't been that long since I saw this bitch last. "Committed. Enjoy ya life, sweetheart," I clicked off the call and blocked her number.

Sitting up on the edge of the bed, I rubbed my bottom lip and thought about the phone call I just hung up on. What was the difference between Lyric and Trenaé? Honesty. Lyric told me up front she had a husband; I was just finding out Trenaé was married only by accident. And if she could invite a random stranger into her bed to give him a piece of herself that should be reserved for her unsuspecting husband, then what made me better than that man?

But didn't Lyric don the same thing? Yes and no. In that truck stop bathroom, I was given a choice and decided to shoot my shot. Had she shot me down, my pride would've been bruised; I'm sure that would've been an awkward ride out here, but I would respect her at the end of the day. I still did. Trenaé, however, was dead to me.

Every time I closed my eyes, I saw her lips on the back of my eyelids. Rubbing my thumb against my middle finger, I felt the impression of her nub, stiff and wet against my knuckles Taking in a deep breath, I smelled her personal perfume, created from her sweet juices still heavily doused throughout my beard. Licking my lips, I tasted her essence; that sweet pineapple she let me suck, nibble, and munch while on the road.

Damn. It was gonna be a long night.

CHAPTER 9
LYRIC

"**O**h you won't be able to make it tonight?" I sighed superfluously in Nolan's ear once he told me he wouldn't be able to make it to New Orleans until the next day. Although I appreciated the gesture, I still had Thaddeus entrenched in my skin no matter how much I tried to scrub him free.

"Nah. Last flight out left thirty minutes after I got off work. I would've never been able to run home, grab a bag, and still make it to the airport. I promise I'll make it up to you, love."

"I really wanted to see you, especially since we didn't spend any time together before I left." I ran my fingers across my lips; the taste of me and Thad's afternoon lingered on my tongue and thoughts. Silently I wondered if sex with my husband would be different from now on.

"Planning your perfect surprise right now for after your meeting, love. This time I…" his words were falling on deaf ears. *This time I want it all…this time I want it all…showing you all the cards…giving you all my heart*…John Legend's *This Time* played on the Tidal app through the speakers as I slept during the ride to New Orleans; I woke up briefly to hear Thad singing the chorus when we crossed Lake Pontchartrain down Interstate 10.

"I'll see you tomorrow, hun, can't wait to see what you have planned," I tuned back into the conversation with my husband when I heard the phone go silent.

"Sleepy baby?"

"Mmhmm. It's been a long day since I woke up in our bed," I yawned.

"Call me in the morning if you get a chance, then," he soothed. "Goodnight Lyric."

"Goodnight, lover," I smiled, envisioning Thad's smile and deep dimples as I told my husband goodbye. Hanging up quickly, I set my alarm before putting my phone on the charger.

Out of nowhere, a clap of thunder shook the house, knocking out power to the small cottage and leaving me in the still, muted space alone. Lightning flashed briefly against the window's pane as the sky opened up, drenching the stifling Louisiana heat into rivers of steaming hot possibilities. The night…this night would have been a perfect backdrop to a sensuous lovemaking session with Thad…Nolan. Lovemaking session with Nolan. My husband.

Looking out over the late-night storm, my thighs ached to be spread once more by the man who drove me to New Orleans from my home in Suwanee, Georgia because I was temporarily scared to get on an airplane. Would Nolan have made that ride if I asked him to? I doubted it. He had an important presentation that day at work that his whole career was riding on, and that took precedence over my safety. Yes, he landed the account and would probably receive a nice bonus, but was that more urgent than the woman who he stood before God and our family to pledge his unyielding love for? In sickness and in health?

Oh, but Thaddeus…mmmm, Thaddeus was still in my head. How does a conversation that started out as a ride to the airport turn into something so much more? I felt like I did when I was a teenager, back when me and my first crush were on the phone talking until our parents told us to hang up and still snuck on the phone afterwards. I blushed thinking back over the past few hours on our trip west. His tongue on my most intimate parts…the taste of his penis…my stomach still twinged slightly thinking about his manhood in my throat.

Stay away from me, Thaddeus. Those words spoken in stupidity echoed through my brain as my hand wandered below my waist. What I should've said was stay with me, Thaddeus. Stay with me…handle me…fuck me, Thaddeus. "Mmmm…make love to me, Thaddeus," I whispered to the pitter-patter of the rain drops pounding against the window pane as my fingers found my wet slit. Grabbing the pillow next to my head, I tucked it between my thighs as I flicked two fingers furiously across my swollen nub. Nudging my sex back and forth into the fluffy material, the look on Thad's face was scrunched up on the back of my lids, right before he was about to shoot his nut inside my womb. "I…ahhhhh, baby…it's coming! IT'S COMING BABY!" I screamed, my juices drenched the pillow that I substituted him for. *Can't leave that here, I'll just have to pay for it, I guess.*

My breathing was shallow as I came down from my euphoric solo ride; I looked around the room for my phone. Checking the time, I saw that it was 1:45 a.m., and I was nowhere near sleepy. The conference began at ten a.m. and was scheduled to go all day. If I didn't fall asleep within the next ten minutes, it wasn't gonna happen. I knew the one person who could put me out quicker than an Ambien; too bad I told him to stay away from me. My pillow and I went to the bathroom to wash up; the way it was looking, we would be going for another round. I had to get some rest.

Damn. It was gonna be a long night.

CHAPTER 10

"Lyric, did you get any sleep last night?" Magda, my receptionist questioned when I Face Timed her at the office to get my messages. "You look exhausted."

"It rained here last night, all that thunder and lightning woke me up and I wasn't able to go back to sleep. Plus the power went out, you know me and heat are not friends," I grumbled, searching around the house for my Louboutin pumps that I pulled out of my suitcase earlier.

"Lost something?"

"Yea, I can't find my shoes," I spoke more to myself than her, heading back into the bedroom to search underneath the oak dresser. "Oh, here they are. But yea, so make sure the team is fully briefed on those reports I emailed you yesterday and we'll discuss the minor discrepancy that almost costed us some major funds. Anything you need from me?"

Magda was scribbling down notes as fast as I could get the words out. "No, everything's good here."

"Great. Wish me luck for this conference, I'm one of the first presenters," I nodded as she waved in the camera.

"Good luck, boss lady! Break a leg!"

"Thanks Magda," I chuckled. "See you soon."

I hung up and called an Uber to head over to the conference center, checking my files for the last time to make sure I had everything I needed. Magda sent over the last few pieces of my presentation, and I triple checked the information for accuracy before my ride arrived. I hoped it was Thad coming to pick me up since he was in the city, but he might've been on his way back to Atlanta by now. Hearing my text ringer ding, I checked first to see how far out my ride was before I checked the message, in case it was something that needed an immediate response.

Good morning love. I know you told me to stay away from you, but I don't want to. Deep down, I know you don't want me to, either. Lyric, I felt you last night. I felt your skin on mine, I felt you rubbing my waves, I heard you call my name. I tasted you…all that sweet cream you saved for me…I got it baby. If you can honestly tell me I haven't crossed your mind none since you slammed the door in my face, I'll leave you alone, like you said.

Frozen in place, I stared at Thaddeus' words, searching my brain for a response. Nolan hadn't sent me a good morning text since…wait…he never sent me a good morning text. We got married because at the time, we had a great vibe. Looking back, I can't say it was love; he was easier to deal with than the other guys that were in my life. We just had…I don't know…a great vibe. Honestly, I can't call it anything else. For once I was at a loss for words; how do I respond? Or do I respond? I always wondered what people meant when they used the term, 'moment of truth.' In this moment it was crystal clear to me after the night I had what my truth was. I could lie to the world about my feelings for him, but I couldn't lie to my heart.

You have crossed my mind. But…

The notification for my Uber dinged, letting me know my ride was outside. Grabbing my Prada portfolio, I tossed my phone and iPad in the bag next to it as I dug around for the key to the tiny cottage. Doing a quick check through the house, I made sure there were no faucets dripping or lights on before running out to my waiting Uber. Jumping in the car quickly, the Uber driver took me to the Marriott. Rehearsing the speech for my presentation as we rode along the banks of the Mississippi River, I put everything going on outside of work in the back of my mind and put my game face on. The company spent a lot of money on this finance conference; as there were a lot of changes going on throughout the airline that we all needed to be briefed on, and I was a part of the team leading the change.

Stepping out of the vehicle, I greeted my co-workers with a big smile, handshakes were abundant as representatives from all over the world gathered for our yearly company-wide meeting. Catching my bosses' attention, my heart sank as he walked over to me. He wasn't a horrible boss, I kind of liked Dimitri. I didn't want him to see the lack of sleep in my eyes and send me home to get some rest. It took a lot for me to get on equal footing with my male counterparts, and I was determined to stay.

"Lyric. Everything ok?"

"Dimitri, I'm well. How was your trip?"

"Relaxing," he smiled politely. *I'm sure it was, when you staying in the penthouse suite at a five star hotel in New Orleans, everything would be peachy.* "And you?"

Well fucked, thanks for asking. "My ride was great, thank you," I smiled politely, my pussy moistening at the memory from yesterday. Thad…oh shit. I forgot to send the message from earlier. "Can you excuse me, Dimitri? I don't wanna be rude, but I have to go set up for my presentation."

"Yes, yes, please," he shooed me inside. "Make me proud, Lyric!" he called out behind me. Waving my arm behind me, I rushed off to the A/V room to hook my iPad up to the projector with my phone in hand. Hitting send, I tucked my device back in my bag and focused back on work for the rest of the day.

CHAPTER 11

I swear I hear you voice driving me insane

How I wish that you would call…to sayyy heyyy ayeee

Do I ever cross your mind, anytime

Do you ever wake up reaching out for me

Do I ever cross your mind, anytime

I miss you…

Me and Brian McKnight sung the hell out of that song as I hit the interstate that stretched across the eastern end of Lake Pontchartrain. I knew I shouldn't have sent her that text, but she needed to know how I felt. She needed to know how I spent my night tossing and turning, sleep not blessing me until the sun peeked over the horizon and even then, only staying for a few hours. She needed to know I wouldn't be able to rest until I tasted her one more time, felt her clit sliding between my teeth; her sex blessing me with her nectar, sticky and viscous as it slipped through my fingers.

When I sent the message, I knew she'd respond. My confidence began to dwindle as time ticked by slowly, after thirty minutes with nothing from her I gave up. Packing my plastic shopping bag from Wal Mart, I headed out of New Orleans. I debated going to the ninth ward to see my mother's sister and the rest of the family, then changed my mind. *Fuck this shit.*

I was almost in Biloxi when she responded to my text, and she hadn't finished her thought when she sent it. 'But'? What was that supposed to mean? 'But' she was scared to give her all to me? 'But' she didn't want to hurt my feelings? 'But' she was masturbating to Cum With Me Volume Six on RedTube so she'd call me later? What the fuck was a 'but'?

Snatching my phone from the holder, I began typing a long, furious message to respond to her 'but'. Speeding down the interstate, I was so focused on my phone that I didn't see the eighteen-wheeler that had come to a complete stop in the middle of the road. By the time I looked up, it was too late…

ΛΛΛ

"Looks like he's coming to," I heard a voice followed by the worst pain I ever felt in my life.

"Praise God. Considering the damage caused to the truck on impact, that seatbelt and airbag saved his life. I've seen people…"

"Shhh, his eyes are opening," a male voice shushed the second person as I struggled to open both lids. "Sir? Sir, how are you feeling?"

"Like I've been crumpled into a ball and kicked down a flight of stairs," I responded. My back ached, my legs felt like noodles, and my head was about to pound out of my skull. "Where am I?"

"Sir, you're in Biloxi, Mississippi," the older white nurse comforted soothingly. "Can you tell us what happened? Do you remember?"

I averted my eyes away from her grandmotherly face, trying to remember why I was in a hospital in Biloxi. Staring at the hospital's drab striped wallpaper, I focused on the bundle of fake grapes that broke up the repetitive pattern every so often. "No."

"Sir, do you know your name? The police were unable to find your personal effects," the doctor spoke softly, placing his hand gently on my shoulder.

I didn't want to tell them I had no idea who I was, I was still trying to figure that out myself. "How…how long have I been here?"

"You were airlifted here from the accident scene almost two weeks ago," the concerned nurse spoke first. At least, I hoped it was concern in her voice. This WAS Mississippi, since I didn't know what was going on, I didn't wanna come up missing.

"And ain't nobody came looking for me?"

"Not yet. Now the state patrol said the car was registered to a Thaddeus Monroe from Stone Mountain, Georgia. Do you remember if that was your car you were driving?"

"What kind of car was it?"

"A uhmm…" he pulled a small notebook from his white coat and flipped through a couple of pages. "…a 2020 Ford Taurus? Black with tinted windows? Does that sound familiar?"

"Can you get me some ice water please? My throat feels like I swallowed a squirrel," I turned to the nurse and asked quietly, ignoring the doctor's questions. I might not remember who I was, but I knew an illegal interrogation when I heard one.

"Are you hungry, sweetie? Do you think you can eat something?" she questioned, sitting the water down on the table in front of me. Pouring a cool cup of the cold liquid, she dropped a straw just inside the rim and held it up to my lips to drink. If it was poison in it, I didn't care, because it felt good going down my throat. "I can get you some applesauce just so you'll have something on your stomach."

"Yes ma'am, applesauce will be fine," I replied, turning away from the male doctor. Shaking his head, he clucked his tongue and walked out of my room. As I stared out the window, I nodded my own head, knowing he was trying to set me up. He didn't refer to my chart not once, nor did he give me an inkling of why I had been here for the past two weeks. Was I coming out of a coma? Did I have any internal bleeding? Was my brain ok? Bitch ass pigs.

Last thing I remembered was waking up at this one chick house that lived out in Snellville. Women flocked to me like a moth to a flame…*like a moth to a flame…I can't stay away*…why was that song stuck in my head? I couldn't remember.

Ol' girl in Snellville didn't want me to drive that night, but after we spent the day cashing out in Buckhead, she gave me the pussy and I had to go get my money back up. Some days I drove Uber, other days I did the Postmates thing, and other times I did Uber Eats. All that was on top of performing at a few hole in the wall spots around the city. I wasn't a dope boy, nor was I a runner, so I didn't know what Super Cop was insinuating when he started questioning me about my whip. I worked my ass off the legal way, just because the boy had Georgia plates didn't make me a hot boy. I can't stand these small town cops.

The nurse, who wrote her name on the dry erase board next to my bed, so I knew she was Phyllis, came back with my applesauce, shutting the door gently behind her. "I made sure it was cold, too," she soothed, tucking a small white towel from the bathroom underneath my chin before she scooted a chair next to the bed closer to where I laid and began to feed me. "Is that better?"

"Mmhmm," I nodded, opening my mouth slightly for her to push the spoon inside. "Thank you."

"You're welcome, son," she scooped another spoon and slid it inside of my mouth again, each bite the same as the first. "Please don't think I'm going to try anything that would cost me my license with you if I get caught," she began. "When they brought you in here, we didn't know if you were gonna make it or not. You had a broken collarbone and a concussion; the doctor thinks that was because you bumped your head some kinda way against the windshield. All that glass we washed out of your face…umph, umph, umph. I'm glad you pulled through."

"Miss Phyllis, I didn't think that at all. I already saw that wedding ring on your finger…" *we're a team…sent to me by God*…a woman's voice that sounded like an angel floated through my ears. "Did you hear that?" I paused mid-sentence.

"Hear what?"

"Nothing. Maybe it was coming from one of the other rooms," I resolved absently, more to myself.

"My hearing isn't what it used to be son; I apologize."

"No, you good Miss Phyllis. Like I was saying, I didn't think nothing of it. Most nurses take their job seriously and ain't in here trying to come up off their patients."

"You remind me so much of my son," she continued, wiping the corner of my mouth. "He was about your age when he died on that same stretch of I-10."

"My condolences to you, sorry to hear that," I replied, shaking my head as she offered me another spoon. I never thought I would get full off some applesauce.

"Thank you. Is there anyone I can call for you? Any family here in Mississippi?"

"I got family in New Orleans; my auntie lives in the Ninth Ward."

"Oh, down where the levees broke?"

"Three blocks down the street."

"And they got out? Lawd chile, your family is blessed!" she fanned herself, sitting back in her chair and giggling as she touched her forehead, chest and both shoulders in the sign of a cross with her right hand.

"My auntie was in Maryland at the time, we had the family reunion up in Annapolis that year. Her house gone, but a bunch of us came down and helped Habitat for Humanity build her a brand new one. She was one of the blessed ones." I thanked God every day for sparing my family, and still prayed for those who weren't as lucky even though it happened almost sixteen years ago. A lot of the kids I played with when I came down to visit my aunt during summer break were gone on to glory, as my grandmother would say.

"What's your aunt's name?"

I gave her my mother's sister's information and we talked for a little while longer before she told me she'd try and Google my people. I thanked her for her conversation as well as an update on what happened to me.

Grabbing the small remote control for the TV from the nightstand, I flipped through the channels, wondering if either of my cousins dropped some of them thangs in my trunk without my knowledge. My memory was coming back to me in pieces as I chilled with the nurse, so I knew I was Thaddeus Monroe. The black Taurus was mine, I had great credit to match my work ethic.

Back in Memphis, I was one fourth of a blues quartet; the buzz in the industry was that I plucked them guitar strings like a young B.B. King, even though I was barely thirty. That's all I heard growing up in South Memphis on the weekends down in the bottoms; it was either that or that dirty south bounce music. Memphis had enough up and coming rappers still trying to be Eightball and MJG, looking for that same love 3-6 Mafia got back in the day. I met a lot of people in my line of work; from grandmas still looking for the hoochie coochie man to young black professionals still hanging on to the music from their childhood when they snuck a capful of moonshine and swore they was drunk. But the white girls? The white women went CRAZY when they heard me strum them strings on that electric guitar!

Can you taste it now….the scent of pineapples filled my nostrils as the voice spoke again inside my head. Was I opening for somebody down in New Orleans? My band was well known throughout the delta, it was possible. But damn, after two weeks I'd think Shawn, Carl and Ray would be looking for me at the least to make sure I was straight when I didn't make it back to Georgia. Maybe it was one of our many, many groupies that wanted to fuck a star. I wasn't as big as the greats, but I was well known. I didn't know whose voice was coming back to me in fragments or why, but I was gonna find out as soon as I was well.

CHAPTER 12
LYRIC

Three days in New Orleans at conference after conference with a bunch of finance majors turned corporate, myself included. If I had to do another ice breaker or group breakout session, I was gonna scream. On the upside, my presentation went well also, the vice president of finance came and praised me about my hard work and research.

I checked my phone during each break to see if Thad responded to my text, but he hadn't. At the very least, I was expecting a 'but what?' Nothing. Guess that paragraph he sent was just that: an empty paragraph with no meaning.

Nolan finally flew down on our last day, and that surprise he hyped up to be so spectacular was nothing more than dinner on Canal Street. Afterwards, we had boring sex in the small cottage where I faked an orgasm after he shuddered his seed inside of me, more of an afterthought than actual love from my husband. Figuring it was because I was still high on Thaddeus, I shook it off as him being nervous, especially since it had been a few months since we made love.

"Lyric?" he called out from the bedroom as I showered alone. Again.

"Yes, honey?"

"Do you love me?"

Stepping out the shower dripping wet with soap covering the upper half of my body, I walked back in the bedroom with water trickling from my fingertips. "Of course I do, love. Why would you ask me that?"

"I'm just saying." He sat up and fluffed his pillows before laying back down to focus in on my body language. "You didn't seem like you were into making love to your husband."

"Tha…that's ridiculous." Hoping he didn't hear my almost slip of the tongue, I waved him off, turning around to walk back into the bathroom to finish my shower. "I always come straight home to you, don't I? Rarely go out with my friends…you can't even come get me from the bar the one time every six months I do go out," I grumbled. "Still and all, I'm married. I remember my vows."

"I vow to trust and value your opinion. To always treat you as my best friend and equal. To be your biggest cheerleader when it seems like no one is on your team.

More importantly, I vow to love you for the rest of my days," he recited my vows back to me. "Can you say that you've kept these vows, Lyric?"

"Where is this coming from?" I rinsed the soap from my body, turning the shower off and wrapping up in a towel.

"Three thousand, six hundred and sixty-three days we've been married, Lyric. Yes, I might've made some mistakes over the years, but I've always took care of home."

"Have you, Nolan? What about our anniversary?"

"Look Lyric, I know you had plans for our tenth wedding anniversary, but if I didn't take that business trip, we wouldn't be able to live the life we've become accustomed…"

"The life YOU'VE become accustomed to," I interrupted. "YOU wanted the big house in Suwanee, the big EMPTY house in Suwanee might I add. YOU wanted to wait before we had kids, 'let's travel, let's work, let's build a nest egg first.' Does any of that sound familiar, Nolan?"

"That's not the conversation we're having, Lyric!" I heard the anger beginning to build in his tone. "Right now, today's debate is about whether or not you've kept your vows! Whether or not you're still in MY corner! Whether or not YOU LOVE ME, LYRIC!"

"YES NOLAN! YES, I STILL FUCKING LOVE YOU! Now can we drop this?"

"We can drop it," he began moving around underneath the covers, finally pulling out his boxers and dropping them to the floor. "Now come over here and rah-rah-rah your mouth on this dick."

"EXCUSE ME, NOLAN? WHAT DID YOU JUST SAY?"

"You heard me. Your job as my wife is to keep my stomach full and my balls empty. Since you ain't cooked in the past year and my balls still tight, the least my wife can do is swallow my meat."

I stood in utter shock, mouth dropped open and listened to my straight-laced husband say things like 'swallowing his meat' and his balls were tight. I was more floored at him telling me to rah-rah-rah my mouth on his dick…his DICK. Nolan never called his penis his dick as long as I'd known him, who he been DM'ing on Adult Friend Finder? "Nolan please," I walked to the dresser to grab my body oils, preparing to rub myself down when I felt a hand on my forearm.

"You my wife, use that mouth for what it was intended," he growled, forcing my head down on his soft pecker. Unlike with Thaddeus, I was disgusted. Opening my mouth as he stuffed his limp penis across my tongue, I bit down on the head semi roughly. "AAAAHHHH! What the fuck you doin'!"

"Get the fuck outta my cottage, Nolan! Go your ass home, talking that crazy shit to me! What the fuck is wrong with you!"

"What the fuck is wrong with me?" he stood up and laughed crazily, clutching his injured manhood in his left hand. "WHAT THE FUCK IS WRONG WITH ME? NAH, WHAT THE FUCK IS WRONG WITH YOU! That pussy ain't NOTHING like I left it! I'm putting a chastity belt on yo' muthafuckin ass, that's what the fuck is wrong with me!" he screamed as the pill bottle fell from underneath the pillow.

We both dived for the bottle, but I was quicker than him and grabbed it first. "Who is Gary Tyson? And why do you have his prescription for Percocet?" I frowned, staring at him with my hand on my hip. "What else in here? Nolan, I don't…oh. OOOOHHHH. You ain't cheating on me with someone, you cheating on me with some THING. And since YOU the one out here stepping outside YOUR vows, now I'M the one who out here bad." Realization and acceptance gut punched me hard, but I wasn't going down. Not for this.

"Gimme my shit, Lyric," Nolan growled, walking slowly towards me. I ducked when he lunged at me, running through the house and opening the front door.

"You want this shit so bad, take your ass outside and go get it!" I used the technique my brothers taught me during my tomboy days and tossed the bottle of pink and white pills outside like a football. Watching the bottle sail through the air and disappear into the sticky Louisiana twilight, Nolan's feet slapping against the hardwood floor came up haphazardly behind me, pushing me against the door as he moved quickly through it.

"You know how much money that is?" he screamed, darting outside still naked as I slammed and locked the door behind him.

How could I not have known? The private investigator never said…he never saw Nolan anywhere but work. Did this Gary Tyson work with him? Or was HE Gary Tyson?

If this happened right under my nose and I had no clue, what else was my husband hiding? Where did this thugged out company vice president of logistics come from? And he wanted me to give him a baby? Bring a baby into this fucked up relationship? No. Hell no.

Gathering Nolan's clothes and stuffing them back in his suitcase, I called the police to report a naked burglar creeping around the property. He needed to sleep it off, and it didn't need to be anywhere near me while he did so, especially not in this rented cottage. I vowed to be his biggest cheerleader, but I wasn't co-signing this mess.

Thaddeus, where are you? Resting my back on the cool door after the police officers left with Nolan's naked ass on the back seat of the cruiser, I wondered where he was, what he was doing. *I need you. I need you bad.*

CHAPTER 13

Nolan sat in lockup for a few days before the judge released him on his own recognizances. By the time he got out, I had flown back home and had the locks changed as well as installed a home security system. I couldn't be married to a pill popper; it was one thing when I didn't know but now I did. All our friends who I always assumed looked at our marriage with envy were in fact giving us looks of pity. EVERYONE knew about Nolan's little 'habit', I was the only one in the dark.

Now that the secret was out, the wives of Nolan's colleagues extended invitations to their exclusive parties 'for the wives'. I didn't know what these women had going on, but I politely declined each one; I had to get my life and marriage on track. IF I decided Nolan and I should still be married after his betrayal.

Growing up, my parents instilled in me and my brothers that any lasting relationship, whether it was a long term commitment, marriage, family, whatever those two people call it, takes a lot of forgiveness. One of my favorite aunts was married, I think five times, and had a lot of men in and out of her life that we called 'uncles'.

Mama used to always say her sister just couldn't get it right; as soon as that man did something she didn't like, she was gone. I'm not talking about something small, like he couldn't let the toilet seat down; more like if he lost the job he had when they met and didn't have another one in a month, she was gone. 'Uncle' Tony had a kid show up out of the blue that was from a relationship ten years before he knew my Aunt Theresa; by that weekend he was replaced with 'Uncle' Maxwell who ended up liking men. I always heard Mama on the phone with her baby sister telling her to talk to the man, but if it wasn't Aunt Theresa's way, she wasn't trying to hear nothing else. All those good men she had (with the exception of Uncle Maxwell, that wasn't her fault), and she ended up dying from a stroke in that big house alone. The coroner said she'd been dead for at least a week before the mailman smelled a foul odor coming from the house when he went to deliver her a package.

I didn't want to be like Aunt Theresa, but I also wasn't gonna be in a relationship where I allowed my husband to live a secret life as a crackhead and condone his actions. Addiction aside, he WAS a good man who provided. He did everything he promised he'd do before we got married, and although we weren't millionaires, we were comfortable. I knew there were women out there that would snatch Nolan right up, habit or no habit, and stand by his side whether he chose to kick it or not. After ten years, I had to do something to save my marriage. Or I had to at least try.

Hearing the harmonious tune of the doorbell chime in my ears, I headed downstairs to see who was disturbing my peace during my moment of reflection. Briefly checking the camera above the wall panel, I saw it was Nolan looking both melancholy and remorseful. Hitting the speaker button on the panel that activated the camera on his side as well, I wanted to look him in the eyes as we spoke. "Hello Nolan."

"Lyric, I understand why you had me locked up. Sitting in that cell for seventy-two hours, I had some time to reflect on my actions and how we got to this place in our marriage and our relationship," he spoke woefully. "I'm…baby I'm sorry," he dropped his head with his shoulders heaving. "I'm so…I'm so sorry."

"Nolan," I hit the button and allowed him into my space…our space. "I'm sorry that it had to get to this point." Falling to his knees once he stepped inside, he wrapped his arms around my waist and wept his apology into my womb.

"I don't want to lose you, Lyric. You're the best thing that ever happened to me, please don't leave," he sobbed loudly.

"Honey, I'm not going anywhere," I kissed the top of his head, wrapping my arms around his skull and cried with him. "We're gonna get through this, love. We're gonna get through this."

ΛΛΛ

Two weeks had gone by since my New Orleans trip, and my feelings for Thaddeus were diminishing more and more as the hours ticked by. Those first three days while Nolan was in lock-up, I longed to just be held by his powerful arms wrapped around my tiny frame and telling me it would be ok. He himself said our chemistry was off the chain, I couldn't understand at first why now, all of a sudden, he wasn't reaching out. Was he really that upset about that 'but' from my last text?

By the end of that first week, I knew that it was all just talk to get in and stay underneath my pencil skirt. Not only was he sexy, but he did say he played in a blues band in Memphis before he came here. I Googled the name of his band to see if they were playing anywhere soon and I saw all the fans, the five-star reviews, the panties on numerous stages, and the women from all races and backgrounds groping that big…pretty…chocolate…

WOOSAH! I felt my face began to flush as my mouth watered staring at the two hands full of his manhood that the woman with the smile on her face staring at Thaddeus with lust in her eyes obviously wanted to feel between her legs. *Girl, I know exactly what you going through,* I thought to myself staring at the pictures posted on Facebook from their fan page, remembering our trip.

Noticing that someone was monitoring and posting on their page, I typed a quick note saying that I loved Thad M., and was trying to find out if he would be available for a private party I was throwing in a few days. I got back an automated response thanking me for contacting the group and a phone number to call regarding booking. I called and left a message, praying my nerves would be calm when whoever called back to give me an update. Like I said, that was a week ago.

My husband and I decided we needed to see a marriage counselor to work out our differences. With the exception of my parents, I realized that in all the relationships that I knew of, there seemed to be a pattern of cheating behavior. My mother was the product of a one-night stand between my grandparents; I never knew my grandfather. Each of my granny's three daughters had a different father. Grandma passed that behavior down to her three daughters; my Aunt Renee was still looking for love at age fifty-two, saying her friend got married again at the ripe young age of sixty-five, so she still had hope. My mother was the only one who broke the cycle, but hearing some of the fights her and my father went through, she'd gone through it herself over the years.

Not wanting to be the one that revived that negative energy that had a hold on my family, I talked to my brothers and my parents, who all agreed that I had to give my union a shot after ten years. Obviously I loved my husband…but a corner of my heart still held on to the possibility that Thaddeus would reach out. That was a bridge that I would cross when the time came.

Taking an extended vacation from work to sort out my conflicting feelings for both my husband and my secret lover, I began to get ready for the day. Nolan and I had an appointment to see Dr. Rice, and after that we were going to visit an outpatient facility for him to get some help for his addiction. Dr. Rice suggested we go together to choose his treatment, and I couldn't agree with him more. Nolan was embarrassed that he put me in a situation where the mask fell away and I saw him for who he really was, and I admitted that maybe I contributed to his addiction by not always allowing him to lead me in our marriage. We were working through our issues and it was a long road, but it was one we were on together.

I was standing in the middle of our walk-in closet trying to decide between the white dress which, to me, signified the refreshing new marriage we were working towards, or the green pants suit that symbolized the growth in the journey we were on together when my phone rang. Without a second thought, I picked it up as I ran my hand over the blue jumper that still had the tag on it. Maybe I'd wear that. "Lyric Allen speaking, how can I help you?"

"Ms. Allen, you don't know me, but my name is Darius. I found your number on my cousin's phone bill, you're actually the last person he texted. I was just trying to see if you might know where he is?"

"I'm…I'm sorry, you have the wrong number. I don't know anyone named Darius," I flipped through my closet looking for a blouse to wear with the tailored pants I finally decided on.

"No, you…maybe I misspoke. My name is Darius, my cousin's name is Thaddeus," the male voice stopped me in mid flip.

"Thaddeus?"

"Yea."

"What…what did you say this call was regarding?" I dropped everything to focus on his words.

"I said my cousin is missing and you're the last person he texted. Do you know where he is? Hello? Miss Allen? Hello?"

The maid found me in the middle of the floor in my walk-in closet ten minutes later, hearing that Thaddeus was missing and I was the last person that he was in contact with was too much for me. All this time I thought I meant nothing to him and he was actually…oh my God. It had been two weeks, where was he? I felt light-headed, the closet started spinning slowly before picking up speed and I couldn't…I couldn't...

Feeling the churning in my stomach, I felt the bile as it began rising in my throat before I fainted.

CHAPTER 14
THADDEUS

"We been worried sick about you, Thaddy." My aunt called me by the nickname that only she was allowed to call me. Anybody else who tried to call me Thaddy might get punched in the mouth. "Your mama called ev'ry hospital and jail in Georgia lookin' fa' ya!"

"I'm jus' glad the nurse here called y'all," I thanked Miss Phyllis for the millionth time for getting in contact with my people. Sitting in the hospital for three months with no visitors, knowing your family is big enough to populate a small town with just your cousins, aunts, and uncles will have you feeling some type of way. After she Googled my family, she realized where she recognized me from; we did plenty of shows in Biloxi, Itta Bena, Greenville, all over the state. Half the student body at Mississippi Valley State University knew EXACTLY who I was. All she asked for in repayment was my autograph and a pic. That was the least I could do, considering what she'd done for me. The state police closed their investigation; being from South Memphis, quite naturally

I'm suspicious of all law enforcement. Buddy was just doing his job.

"Well, the insurance comp'ny called here looking fa' you 'bout ya car," she began. I knew what that was all about, she wanted to see how much money I was getting back and how much she would get for being the contact person. "I tole them you wuz in da' hospital still."

"I'm bout to call them now, I gotta get a rental to go home." The police told me that although I was the one that hit the back of the truck, the driver was actually at fault. If I wasn't the one that hit him, someone else would have anyway. I was in negotiations with the company that he was hauling for to settle the case out of court. I already told their lawyer I wasn't settling for anything less than seven figures; anything less and we could go see the judge, who I was sure would give me eight or more.

"Don't forget about those that helped you git where you are now," she hissed in the phone; I knew the double meaning of that statement all too well.

"I gotchu, auntie," I replied before hanging up. I loved my family, but there was a reason I didn't go see them when I was in New Orleans.

Spending three months in the hospital, I had about 99% of my memory back. I recall being in the city, spending the night in a small room, and driving over the lake to get both in and out of the city. The only thing my mind was still blocking out was the owner of the voice that popped up during the most random times. While waiting for my discharge papers, I was in the shower lathering up when her voice told me my cum tasted so sweet. Last night I was jolted out of my sleep when her voice screamed happily for me to fuck her. Whoever this woman was haunted me for the past three months; I had to put a face to the voice.

The insurance company got me right: the manager from Enterprise called me at the hospital and even came through to pick me up so I could do my paperwork and drive home. We went through the truck driver's insurance company; so I was approved for a one-way back to Georgia. They even replaced my car; the guy from Nalley Ford in Sandy Springs was waiting to get me into another Taurus, same color, same model year…they were tinting my windows as we spoke.

I had to stop off and grab another iPhone to replace the one destroyed in the accident. Since none of my expenses were on my dime, I upgraded and got the latest model out.

Scanning the receipt to my email so I could submit it to the insurance, I logged into my iCloud to see what I'd been up to those couple of days I was in the Big Easy.

First thing I did was log into my Uber account; I forgot to cash my earnings before I hit the road. Seeing they included that money in my weekly deposit a few weeks ago, I then checked to see if my last ride tipped me. "Five hundred dollars for a tip?" I stopped walking to make sure I saw it correctly. "Where the hell did I go?" Scrolling to see the trip details, I felt my eyebrow raise reading that I drove from Suwanee to New Orleans. "Why would I…"

Memories of that morning suddenly flooded my head, now I knew who she was. Lyric. Closing the Uber Driver app, I pulled up my text messages next as her voice screamed in my head for me to stay away from her. I saw her last message to me: *You have crossed my mind. But…* My mind went back to that night…that hot, sticky night on a side street in New Orleans where I stood with the woman who could very easily be the first Mrs. Monroe:

"I'll text you the address to where you'll be staying and tip you on the app," she snatched her luggage away and fumbled with the key in the lock. "We had fun, but now it's over. Stay away from me, Thaddeus."

Gripping my phone in my hand, I stormed to the rental car with HER on my mind. The lil' pussy from the night before didn't matter no more; I barely remembered her name. Lyric, though…Lyric…I was gonna send her ass a…

Slamming the door to the rental, I hit the push button start on the Dodge Challenger when my new phone vibrated with a text message. Since Apple sent the oldest message first, I knew the messages were in chronological order as they came in. Opening the envelope icon on my phone, I read the first message:

Thaddeus, I'm sorry. I was wrong, I was the asshole. Please call me, please? I need you, Thaddeus. I need you, please.

The number wasn't familiar to me, but judging by the messages, they had to be from Lyric. "I wasn't there…baby I'm sorry I wasn't there…" I beat the steering wheel as I read her words.

You were right, we do have chemistry. I tried fighting it, but now, now I know that you're the one for me. Please call me so we can talk, I just…I just wanna hear your voice.

Thaddeus please don't do me like this. Please. I'm sorry, I'm so…so sorry. Please call me, please.

Haven't heard from you, just wanna make sure you're ok.

Ok. I get it. I won't bother you anymore. Have a nice life.

I didn't know whether I should reach out and explain what happened, or if I should just wish her well too. The old folks said if you love something, set it free. If it comes back it's yours. If it doesn't, it never was. Lyric set me free, did she want me to do the same? Did I want to do the same?

Once I connected the device to the Bluetooth, my phone rang almost immediately. Checking the console screen, the number looked vaguely familiar, but it wasn't Lyric. "Yea."

"Cuzo?" my ace, Darius, questioned throughout the car's speakers.

"Whaddup, cuz."

"Shit, I thought yo' ass was somewhere locked up!" I chuckled to myself at the relief in his voice. "Auntie called yo' mama an' told her you got yo' self in some accident down in Biloxi."

"Yea, that shit was crazy, bro. I'm jus' thankful to the man upstairs that I'm still here."

"Yea, big up to the big homie for sparing yo' life like that, man," he reiterated. "I been callin' ev'rybody in yo' iCloud tryin' to fine out what happened to you."

"How you got access to MY iCloud, my G?"

"Yo, you forgot when you started doin' Uber you synced yo' cloud to mine so in case somethin' happened, somebody would know where yo at?"

"If that's the case, you should've known where I was an' came out here, bro!" I yelled, frustrated that my cousin knew where I was this whole time and didn't come check on me.

"Actually, I didn't. When you started messing wit' ol' girl from Snellville you unsynced me, but for some reason I still had access to your phone book and text messages. I called that last number you texted and a female answered the phone. Who is Lyric Allen, cuz?"

"You talked to Lyric? What she say?" I ignored him being nosy, what was more important to me was what she had to say about us.

"First she acted like she ain't know what I was talkin' bout," he began. "I had to cut into her ass."

"What you mean, 'you had to cut into her ass'?"

"Aye, she was like 'I 'ont know what you talkin' bout.' I jus' had to tell her straight up, 'look bitch, my cousin missing an' I think you know where he at. Yo' ass betta tell me sumthin' fo' I come chop yo' ass up into little pieces," he growled in the phone.

"Darius. Cousin. Tell me you did not say that to her."

"What? Fuck her, shit, you was missin'! I said what I had to say!"

"And how far did that get you, my G?"

"She hung up on me. That's another thing: I need her address. I'm 'bout to go over her house, man…don't no bitch hang up the phone in my face!" he yelled angrily.

"Look, muthafucka. You lucky I ain't comin' ova YO' house right now! Don't talk to no woman I'm dealin' wit' like you talkin' to these strippers/thots/bucket headed/deadbeat bitches you fuck wit'!"

"Cuz, this me! You gonna talk to me like that ova a bitch?"

"Watch ya muthafuckin' mouth, my G. Don't call her no mo', matter of fact, lose her numba," I grumbled before hanging up in his face. I had to reach out after finding out this muthafucka said THAT to her.

Hitting talk on her number, I watched the screen as the call connected and I listened to her phone ring. I made it up in my mind that I'd just explain to her what was going on, so at the end of the day, she knew I didn't give up on her or us.

"Thaddeus? Please tell me you're ok," she rushed, not bothering to say hello.

"I'm ok, Lyric." Judging from the concern in her tone, I knew she needed to hear those words first. I didn't know what Darius told her for real, but hearing her sigh with relief, it didn't matter. "How are you?"

"Better now that I know you're alive," she breathed. "Can I see you? Are you home?"

"Almost there; I'm passing through Columbus right now. What happened with your…"

"Thaddeus, I have so much to tell you. Please, can we spend some time together?"

"We can do whatever you want, love. Where you wanna meet?"

"I'll get us a room…" she began.

"Correction: I'LL get us a room. Where you wanna go?"

"You sure?" she questioned cautiously. "I don't mind…"

"So, where you wanna go, again?"

"The W in Buckhead?" she questioned hopefully.

"Good choice. I'm cool with the bartender at the rooftop bar. I'll get us a room out there an' we can talk, aight?"

"Ok."

"Wait, I thought you didn't like hotels?"

"Not ALL hotels, just the ones in New Orleans," she giggled. "I don't mind the W."

"You crazy," I chuckled with her. "I'll text you the room number when I get out there, aight?"

"Ok. Thad, I'm really happy that you're ok."

"Me too. See you soon, love."

"Bye baby." She was cheesing when she hung up, I heard it all in her voice. I couldn't wait to see her again.

CHAPTER 15
Lyric

"Thank you Jesus, Mary and Joseph," I sighed, disconnecting our call. Thaddeus was ok…he was alright. I could exhale without taking in a deep breath and holding it in. Considering all that happened since the morning when the maid found me on the floor, I was happy to know Thaddeus was still alive. I had so much to tell him about me and Nolan. Never in a million years would I have thought that situation would play out like it did, but everything happens for a reason. Sitting here thinking about it had me feeling some type of way.

Before the call…

I felt fine, I knew the real reason I was passed out on the plush carpet in my walk-in closet, but the maid told me that maybe I should lie down for the rest of the day. Initially I resisted, but when she stood in my closet and refused to let me get dressed, I said fuck it. Stripping out of my pants, I tucked into my bed with only my underwear on and waited for my husband to come home. Nolan said he had to run to the office real quick to fill out the paperwork for his leave, and he wouldn't be gone long.

Somewhere during the afternoon, I fell asleep and was dreaming about me and Thad when I heard my FaceTime ringer go off. The only person that video called me was my receptionist Magda, and since she knew I was out on personal leave, a call from her must've meant it was important. Fishing my phone out from the drawer on my nightstand, I fluffed my hair a little so I didn't look too haggard, and hit the button to answer. I couldn't unsee the scene that popped up on my camera if I rewinded the last thirty seconds of my life and hit erase.

Magda's iPhone X was mounted on her nightstand next to her bed; I'm guessing her retina scanner picked up her pupils at some point during her afternoon tryst. Pills and a white powdery substance covered her black sheets as I heard moans and grunts of passion and sexual release coming from the phone's speaker. A figure underneath the covers rose up and jerked rapidly back and forth as Magda screamed for someone to go deeper. What I assumed was an arm reached out and swiped the pill bottles from the nightstand, knocking over a bottle of clear alcohol, before fumbling around until the hand found a pill. Throwing the satiny sheet from the top of its head, my hand fluttered to my throat when I saw who was underneath the covers. My husband.

"Mmm…baby why you stop?" Magda purred from underneath him, tapping a small glass vial. Tracing a line of what had to be cocaine, considering the circumstances, from the top of her breast down to her nipple, she smiled and wiggled her chest gently from side to side.

"You got this bitch as your screensaver? I know you love your boss, but how you get a picture of her like this?" he grabbed the phone from the stand and turned it towards her shocked face.

"No, *mi amor*, that's your…"

"Lyric?" he cackled that same demented laugh from when we were in New Orleans before sniffing the line of coke from her titty. "Watch what your little assistant be doing when you ain't around." Taking the small vial of cocaine from her shaky hand, he poured the rest on his erect manhood in a line from the base to the tip. "Come take care of Daddy, baby."

"Lyric, I can explain," Magda spoke shakily into the camera, tears streaming down her face before Nolan grabbed the back of her head and snatched her neck back.

"FUCK HER! I SAID COME TAKE CARE OF DADDY!" Nolan screamed, forcing her mouth open and shoving himself inside. Bending his leg at a ninety-degree angle, he defiled her over and over until he was satisfied. Pushing her head back down on the mattress, he held the phone up again and smiled maniacally on the phone's screen. "See Lyric, Magda knows how to take care of her man. That's the nut I was saving for you. Least somebody got it, ain't that right, baby?"

Magda laid on the bed still. Completely still. "Nolan…" I started.

"What, you mad? Or you wanna know why I'm fucking your assistant? Ok," he clapped, hopping up from the bed butt naked, "I came up to your job one day nine months ago and you were in a meeting. I figured I'd wait, wanted to take my wife to lunch, it was kinda early, yatta, yatta, yatta. Magda told me you shouldn't be too long, and offered me a seat. No problem, I know how these meetings go," he was nodding his head up and down while pacing the floor back and forth, high out of his mind. "So, an hour goes by. Fine.

Two hours go by. I'm thinking, "ok, what's going on?" Two hours and fifteen minutes, your little assistant offers me a cup of water, she see I'm mad. Now that's what a woman supposed to do; see her man going through some things and react," he snapped his fingers to emphasize his point.

Magda still hadn't moved a muscle, I wasn't 100% sure, but it didn't look like she was breathing. "Nolan…"

"SHUT UP! DAMN, THAT'S WHY WE IN THIS SHIT NOW! YOU DON'T KNOW WHEN TO SHUT THE FUCK UP!" he screamed. "Now where was I? Oh yea, Magda. So this little spicy Latina that you got working for you brought me some water, and when she handed me the cup, she smiled. You know how long it's been since a beautiful woman smiled at me?"

"Nolan I smile at you all the…"

"NO THE FUCK YOU DON'T! LEMME TELL THE STORY, DAMMIT!"

I took a deep, cleansing breath in and exhaled slowly. "Finish your story then, Nolan."

"After that, we exchanged numbers and talked. I used to sit in my office and talk to her all day. Those days she would leave the office early, telling you she had to go pick up her son? She would call me and we'd talk for hours. Magda ain't even got no kids," he sneered viciously.

"No surprise there," I breathed, picking up my second phone and texting 911. Regardless of what she was doing with my husband, I was sure she needed medical attention. Nolan jerked her head back a little too hard to me, and when he claimed she was pleasuring him on camera, I didn't see her lips move. I've sucked a dick (or two) in my lifetime, so I knew the other person had to be involved some kind of way.

"The first day we met up outside of the office, I took her to dinner and afterwards, she thanked me. She was appreciative. SHE APPRECIATED ME, LYRIC! WHEN IS THE LAST TIME YOU APPRECIATED ANYTHING I'VE EVER DONE? WHEN IS THE LAST TIME YOU'VE THANKED ME FOR KEEPING A ROOF OVER YOUR MUTHAFUCKIN' HEAD, LYRIC?"

"Nolan, I ain't gotta 'thank' you for a muthafuckin' thing. We married. That's what you supposed to do. BOTH of our money has gone into this house, these cars, this furniture, the food in the refrigerator, the forks in the sink, the tissue you wipe your muthafuckin' ass with. I work too," I replied calmly, which was a shock even for me.

"That's the shit I'm talking 'bout right there," he shook his finger at me. "Right there! That smug ass attitude of yours! THAT'S why when Magda offered me a perky to take the edge off, I took it! THAT'S why when she introduced me to coke, I tried it out! THAT'S why when she offered me the pussy, I TOOK IT! And what a fine piece of pussy it was, Lyric! Nothing like that saddity shit you out here rationing out! Naw, Magda give me pussy WHEN I want it, WHERE I want it, and HOW I want it! Your ass? 'You gotta go to therapy, Nolan'," he whined my words, "'You gotta go to treatment, Nolan.' 'We gotta work on our marriage, Nolan.' FUCK YOU AND FUCK THIS MARRIAGE!" he screamed as I heard pounding on the door.

"And that should be the police, Nolan. Had YOU shut the fuck up, your dumb, dope fiend ass would've realized that Magda hasn't opened her mouth not one time since you call yourself telling me everything I don't fucking do. That woman has either overdosed, or your stupid ass snapped her neck trying to prove a point to me, the woman who ain't never done nothing to you but try and love on your ignorant ass. Had I known THIS is who you really were, I would've left you standing in the middle of that houseboat looking like a fucking fool while I went home. Don't drop the soap, cokehead," I spoke quietly as the bedroom door came crashing in behind him before I hung up.

CHAPTER 17

The police arrested Nolan when they went to check Magda and found her unresponsive. By the time the paramedics showed up, it was too late, she died within minutes. After the coroner pronounced her cause of death from asphyxiation exacerbated by a compromised respiratory system, Nolan's lawyer called and informed me that there was no reason for him to go to trial; even if he pled guilty he was still going away for a long time. The police determined the cocaine and prescription drugs in her apartment were his, and charged him separately for each pill. He'd never see the light of day as a free man again in his life.

On the outside, I was a mess. I publicly grieved for my husband and the destruction of our marriage, deciding to become an advocate for the war on drugs. The situation with Nolan forced me to take the blinders off and see my marriage for what it really and truly was: a complex web of drugs, sex, adultery, and lies. We looked great on the outside: power couple with the big house in the suburbs and the picket fence. Soon we'd add a baby to our union to complete the beautiful picture complete with a beach and sunset. The truth was something dark and menacing; if someone looked closer at that proverbial picture, they'd see the smiles were fake, the elbow that should have been on the shoulder was a lot closer to the neck than it should be. We were stifling each other's growth and it was consuming both of us as the minutes to forever slowly dragged on.

But on the inside…behind those closed doors, I was free. I WAS FREE. Free from the doubt, free from the guilt eating me alive, free from it all. Free to love the man I longed to be with, free from the judgement that came with it. God saw my pain and smiled on me by rescuing me from a lifetime of loneliness. I was going to do something I hadn't done in a long time: I was going to church. My mother asked me every day if I'd gone to see my husband behind bars, and I told her no. After what he said to me, go see him? No. Nolan finally got his true feelings for me off his chest, and for that I was glad. Jesus bless Magda's confused soul, but that was who should've been going to support him, not me. Had he not killed her, I was positive she would have.

The house in Suwanee was too big for just me and Nolan, but with him gone, I had to sell it. I didn't want to live there; it was a constant reminder of my marriage that had shattered into pieces right in front of my face. Until I found a place to live, I stayed with my parents in Fayetteville. My parents converted my old room to a guest room, which was fine with me. That first night, my mother tucked me in like she used to when I was younger. I woke up to the smell of bacon, sausage and pancakes the next day. Grabbing my robe, I went in my private bathroom to take care of my morning hygiene before heading downstairs to get some food.

"Good morning, mama," I sang as I walked in the kitchen, kissing her cheek before I sat down to eat. My father had already left for work, I heard the garage door open and shut early this morning before the sun came up. "Is this my plate?"

"Yea, that's yours sweetheart," she turned her back to the stove after flipping the last pancake onto the plate next to the stove. "Mine is right here. Come have breakfast wit'cha mama. We ain't talked in a while."

Looking around for the butter, I grabbed the warm syrup and poured it on my hot stack. "Sure mama, what you wanna talk about?"

"Well Lyric, I'm gonna cut straight through the bullshit and ask you: are you cheating on Nolan?"

"What? MAMA!"

"I went to see my son-in-law the other day, since you hadn't," she sliced a tomato and placed it on top of her eggs. "He told me he didn't think you were being faithful, and that's why he said those things to you. He also said your co-workers called and told him you weren't at the hotel that the company paid for you to be at."

"Mama that doesn't mean I'm being unfaithful," I chuckled. For a second, I thought Nolan had me followed that morning. "What it does prove is that he doesn't pay me any attention, I told him a long time ago the water bugs in the hotels in New Orleans were as big as your hand."

"Hmph," she clucked her tongue and turned sideways in her chair. "I dreamt about fish last night. Haven't had that dream since Yvonne was pregnant."

"Maybe I'm about to get another niece or nephew to spoil," I smiled, demolishing my plate. "Are there any more pancakes?"

"Yea, baby," she smiled in my direction before grabbing the platter of pancakes, placing them in front of me. Forking three more cakes onto my plate, I poured more syrup on my pancakes and started working on my meal.

"Just so you know, neither Yvonne, Denise nor Mari is pregnant."

"Maybe one of Auntie Theresa daughters pregnant," I reasoned. "What month is this? You know they take turns popping out a kid every three months."

"Stop talking about my nieces," my mother snickered. She knew I wasn't lying though.

"Mama, what you trying to say?"

"Your husband is concerned that his drug use might have an adverse effect on your baby," she spoke softly.

"Baby? What baby? Mama, I ain't pregnant."

"Oh no? I know for a fact that plate of yours had four sausages and four pieces of bacon. Not to mention you done reached over here and scraped all the eggs off my plate and that's your sixth pancake. Who ain't pregnant?"

"Wha…ma'am? Mama, I ain't…" I began before looking down at my plate. She was right. "I was hungry, it's been a while…"

"Since you ate, Lyric?"

"Since I've had your cooking," I sulked, pushing my chair away from the table. "Nolan filling your head up with these vicious lies. My own mother. Stay away from him mama, he's toxic."

"Where you going, sweet pea?" she called me the name both my parents used to call me when I was younger. Holding my stomach, I stomped up the steps to get away from her accusations.

"I'm tired, mama. I gotta go lie down."

"Tired from eating, sweetie?" she giggled.

"Mama, I'm not pregnant!" I yelled back down the steps.

ΛΛΛ

Going to see my soon to be ex-husband in the Fulton County jail was bittersweet; a part of me still had slight feelings for him. We did exchange vows before God and our family to love one another in sickness and in health. His sickness, however, was what ultimately tore us apart.

The door opened and the inmates filed in from a separate room. Nolan was the last one to come in, limping with a swollen face and black eye. My heart broke for him, but I couldn't get those words he spoke to me out of my head long enough to do anything other than feel sorry for him.

"I'm glad you came," he stood in front of me with holding his arms open for an embrace, finally having a seat across from me when he realized that wasn't about to happen. "Thank you for coming."

"Nolan, you told my mother I was pregnant?"

"I knew that would get your attention and you would come see me," he snickered gloomily before dropping his head to stare blankly at the circular table. "I just wanted to see you one more time before the judge sentenced me.

Reaching across the table, I rested my hand on top of his. "I don't know how you knew, but I am. I took a test this morning that confirmed it."

Nolan's head rose slowly, turning his face towards me. "What did you just say?"

"I'm pregnant Nolan. We're gonna have a baby." I chuckled bitterly, realization of my situation cutting through my soul with karma's machete. "We're gonna have a baby and I'm gonna be a single parent."

"Who is he?"

"Nolan, please. Not again, ok?"

"I'm serious, Lyric. Is it somebody I know?"

"What are you talking about?"

"I got a vasectomy after we had that first pregnancy scare," he growled through gritted teeth. "I didn't want to ever have to feel the pain of having to view the body of another stillborn baby, so I went and had it done at my doctor's office. If you're saying you pregnant, I know for a fact it ain't mine."

"You and Magda…"

"Was fucking. We never used anything, she was a virgin before me. I ain't have to worry about getting her nor the others…"

"Others? Who else, Nolan?"

"Pregnant. We should've never got married," he shook his head while covering his mouth. "We should've never, ever got married. I came to Atlanta to start my life over, but they kept calling…"

"Who, Nolan?"

"The drugs," he admitted. "I've been an addict since my senior year of high school. Got it kicked back home, but when I came down here and saw how easy they were to get…" his voice trailed off.

"Lemme get this straight, I MARRIED a crackhead?"

"Yea," he nodded while staring off into space. "Yea. I stopped going to meetings, stopped seeing my sponsor. I felt like I was functioning. Magda offered me that Percocet, and it was just like riding a bike when that dope hit my system…"

"Wow. Just…wow. I never would've guessed you of all people."

"Looks can be deceiving, sweetheart," he kissed the back of my hand gently with dry, cracked lips. "It doesn't matter who he is, you have my blessing. I know you not gonna wait for me while I'm in here, and I'm not gonna ask you to. My lawyer says I'm facing 200 years for all that shit they found at Magda's plus they charging me with manslaughter. Just…" he fought back a tear, "…just bring the baby up here to see his or her Uncle Nolan, alright?"

"I can do that," I wept quietly.

"Sell the house. Keep everything in the bank accounts, all I ask is that you send me a couple of dollars for commissary. Can you do that for me, Lyric?"

"I can."

"I got the divorce papers. I signed them and gave them back to my lawyer, that was my only stipulation," he continued. "Make sure the job send you my bonus and pay you out for my benefit time, I had that specifically written in my offer letter when I started."

"Ok."

"Take care of yourself, Lyric," he kissed me on the top of my head as the guard announced visitation was over.

Walking back to my car, I never thought Nolan would tell me he was sterile. He got a vasectomy when I got pregnant four years ago and our baby was stillborn. The doctors swore one of us had a genetic defect and ordered us to take all these tests…but Nolan convinced me they were wrong. I knew it wasn't me; my parents birthed me and three boys, and all of my siblings had children. We weren't working on a baby in New Orleans. We wasn't working on nothing but a nut.

So, since I wasn't pregnant by Nolan, the only other person it could possibly be was…Thaddeus.

CHAPTER 18
THADDEUS

"Look who's here," I greeted Lyric with a tight hug followed by some tongue. "Mmmm, you missed me?"

"I did," she snuggled up to my chest, wrapping her arms around me a little tighter. "Did you miss me?"

"Hell yea," I took her hand in mine, leading her to the couch overlooking the Atlanta skyline. "Those lips, those hips, that mind of yours that's always running a mile a minute," I smiled as I stared in her eyes. "I missed all that."

"You wanna show me how much you missed me?" she questioned, taking two steps back before attempting to pull her dress over her head.

"Nah, baby, let me do that," I put my hand on top of hers, watching slowly while pulling the rest of the dress over her head. My eyes instinctively roamed over each curve; mentally I traced her outline with my eyes, committing it to memory. "Sexy, love."

"Thad, I have something to tell you," she began as I gripped her thighs. I been thinking about this woman's hips, lips, taste…since I remembered us.

"Daddy's gonna keep you here with me, baby," I moaned in her ear. Gently kissing her lips, I moved to her ears repeating my actions pulling her close to me and holding her tightly. Traveling downwards to her neck, I breathed in the anticipation coming off her skin before sinking my teeth into her flesh.

Sucking her neck, I listened patiently as she whispered in my ear how much she loved and needed me…needed be to make love to her. Begging me to make love to her soul, I positioned her on all fours, arching her back in so she could toot that ass up for me. Pulling her panties down with one hand, I stuck my tongue in her pussy sideways while fingering her snatch with the other. Lyric moaned loudly as she drenched my face with her orgasm. I sloshed my fingers in and out of her wet slit, humming on her pussy lips as she whimpered lowly. "Mmm…like that baby?"

"Yes," she breathed. Like that, baby."

My dick was about to tear a hole in my pants, he was ready for some attention too, but I wanted to make sure she was satisfied first. I picked up a strawberry from the bowl next to the couch, flicking my tongue back and forth over the sweet, firm fruit. "Come here, sweet."

"Thad, I wanna fuck," she pleaded. "I want you to shove your dick in this pussy…" she spoke firmly while pulling my pants down. My dick popped out fully erect and smacked her in the face, "…and touch the bottom, like you did when we was on the road." Standing up straight, I snatched her panties all the way off before she straddled me. "Lemme gush this wet all over yo' muthafuckin' dick," she dropped down and started riding my shit like a cowboy.

I gripped her neck as she leaned back with her hands planted firmly on my knees, watching her pussy swallow my dick as I pulled him back slick with her juices. "I'ma have you thinking about this dick all day, you hear me," I grunted. "When you walk in the bathroom to wash that pussy, you gonna want this dick. When you put your clothes back on, you gonna wanna ride this dick. When you driving home, that pussy gonna cum in the car because of this dick. When you get ready for bed, this dick gonna put yo' ass right to sleep. Who pussy is this, Lyric?"

"AAAHHH SHIT!" she growled. "This yo' muthafuckin' pussy…mmmm…."

"You love me, girl?"

"Ye…ye…YESSSS DADDY!" she twisted around and rode my shit backwards. Grabbing her by the throat, I squeezed her neck while biting her shoulder as she bounced up and down. "I'm…I'm…"

Sliding her quickly off my shit, I laid down and flipped her upside down, dipping my tongue back inside her sweet candy, trying to suck the soul out of her as she put her mouth on my manhood, lapping her juice off my shit trying to do the same. "Show him you love him, girl," I stuck my thumb in her other tight hole as her pussy came for me, drowning my face in sweet cum.

"FUUUUCKKK," she moaned, rubbing her mound back and forth over my face as my thumb sank deeper and deeper into her ass.

Switching positions, I had her on all fours, gripping my dick from the base and rubbing the tip back and forth from the top of her clit to the top of her ass to lube her up naturally. Pushing the tip against her booty, I rested the tip against her reluctant hole as she resisted, squeezing her cheeks together at first.

"I don't…I don't do that…" she insisted, trying to run away from me.

"I know, baby," I pulled her closer, palming her titties as the sweat dripped from my face and landed in drops on her back. "Just lemme put the tip in, I promise it won't hurt."

"Thad, I don't know," she tried wiggling out of my grip, but I had her right where I wanted her.

"Just relax, baby," I coached, dipping the tip in her pussy and taking advantage of the fact that she was still ready to fuck. "Relax your muscles, that's the reason why you think it's gonna hurt." Sliding the tip in, I let out a low sigh as her muscle tightened up around my dick. "Mmm, don't that feel good?"

"No," she fussed a little while tightening and relaxing her ass.

"Wait a minute," I pushed him in slowly, reaching around to finger her pussy as she relaxed completely. "What about now?"

"Mmm…now, baby," she moaned as I watched my dick plunge deeper inside her tight hole. Seeing my manhood become slick let me know out the gate that Lyric was an undercover freak, just like I liked 'em.

Sticking my fingers in her mouth, she sucked her juices from my fingers and dipped my hand back inside her slit so she could do it again. "Give Daddy that cum, baby. Give it to me," I whispered in her ear, digging deeper into her sticky crevice until she exploded from BOTH holes. I didn't know a woman could cum in her ass the same as she could out of her pussy.

"OH MY GOD! THADDEUS!" she threw her head back and wailed, all the while still fucking. "gimme…oh baby, gimme…"

"This what you want?" I grabbed her hair and shot my babies straight into her stomach. We was just gonna have to explain to her husband that a real G got the pussy, he was just gonna have to understand.

"Yes…YES! Oh…oh…ooooohhh yes!"

"You gonna have to start giving Daddy this pussy on a regular," I whispered in her ear, rubbing her hair and kissing her face as she collapsed on my chest. "Hubby will be aight."

"Thad, I got something to tell you," she whispered sleepily.

"What's that, sweetheart?"

"I'm...I'm..." her light snores came before she tucked her head completely in the pillow.

Wanna put my fingers through your hair, wrap me up in your legs, and love you til your eyes roll back, I'ma put you to bed...bed...bed...lemme put you to bed...bed...bed, I smiled, pulling the covers up to her chin before kissing the top of her head. Going in the bathroom to wash up, I tiptoed quietly back in the room when I heard her mumbling in her sleep.

"A baby," she tossed and turned in slumber. "A baby, mama. Me and Thad gonna...gonna have a baby..."

"Lyric," I gently shook her awake. "You know you talk in your sleep?"

"I wasn't asleep," she smiled.

"So...we...what about..."

"I promise I'll tell you everything later. Right now, I wanna make love to my baby daddy," she snickered.

"You do that," I joined her underneath the covers. "And while you doing that, I'll be making love to my wife."

"Really?"

"Really. You giving me my first baby, first woman I can truly say I fell in love with in a matter of hours…I can't see myself without you. I never believed when my people used to say they found a woman that gave them a love that would never dilute, no matter what. To me, that was impossible. Meeting you that day, talking to you…you gave me your body in a way that I ain't never felt before. I love you, Lyric. Knowing that you carrying my baby…it's my job to make sure my queen and my little prince or princess stay flawless at all times. I can't do that unless you my wife."

"Thad, I love you too," she stared me deep my eyes, and I saw her soul. "You make passion, love and madness combine and run through my veins when we're together. When I'm with you I feel like I have that 'everything or nothing' type of love. You are my place of peace, I can be myself with you. I thought I had that before, but now I realize…you. You are my destiny, Thaddeus."

"And you are mine, love," I kissed the tip of her nose. "This is where it begins for US. Not your husband, not my past…none of that has any bearing on US. Right now," I palmed her womb, "right now this is a responsibility that we both gonna have to accept, happily and with love. Truth be told: I couldn't ask for a better partner, soulmate, or friend to share this miracle with. Lyric you are everything I want in a relationship, and more than I knew was possible. I wanna spend the rest of my life making you happy."

"Can you…can you repeat that when we go in front of the wedding officiant?" she cried tears of happiness.

"I'll give you something better," I wiped her face with the crook of my finger. "You ready to take this ride with your man?"

Ready as I'll ever be," she pressed her lips against mine. Wrapping my arm around her shoulders, I knew in that moment I would never let her get away from me again.

The End

Thanks for reading! I appreciate you for taking the time to download and enjoy my work! If you enjoyed Thad and Lyric's story, can you do me a favor and leave a review? I love feedback: good, bad or indifferent! Thanks!

Get short stories from Monreaux authors that'll have you BEGGING for the full novel! Join our forum and chat with other members about Mia and Charles' story, Flawless! Haven't read it yet? It's not on Amazon, you gotta join our mailing list: www.monreauxpublications.com

Read Atif and Cary's urban love story NOW! Grab my latest two book series here: https://amzn.to/37zutz8

Follow me on social media!

Facebook: http://facebook.com/authorfatimamunroe

http://facebook.com/groups/ReadingWithFatima

http://facebook.com/groups/thebookishnook

Instagram: http://instagram.com/fatima_munroe

LinkedIn: http://linkedin/in/monreauxpublications

Twitter: http://twitter.com/fatima_munroe

Goodreads: http://goodreads.com/fatimamunroe

Clubhouse: @fatimamonreaux

HAVE YOU READ A BOOK FROM MONREAUX PUBLICATIONS?

Carols,
SNOW AND
MISTLETOE
A CHRISTMAS LOVE ANTHOLOGY
TAMIKA BROWN,
RENA WILLIAMS, FATIMA MUNROE

Monreaux Publications
Let Me
LOVE YOU
TAMIKA BROWN
Monreaux Publications

Monçeaux
Revelations
JAMYE DEBARDELEBEN

JOIN US.

We're accepting manuscripts in the following genres:

Women's Fiction
Urban Fiction
Street Lit
Romance
Erotica
Paranormal Romance
LGBTQ
Interacial
Thrillers
Sci-Fi
Children's

Send your first four chapters to:
fatima@monreauxpublications.com

Allow 48 - 72 hours for a response.

K. BURNS
MONREAUX PUBLICATIONS
MY BROTHER'S KEEPER

MONREAUX PUBLICATIONS PRESENTS
DESTRUCTIVE Obsession
VIVIAN BLUE

www.ingramcontent.com/pod-product-compliance
Lightning Source LLC
Chambersburg PA
CBHW020719160726
47993CB00006B/2271